Dying To Be Straight! Too

Michael D. Beckford

SpeakPublishing International

"Reeling in One Reader at a time."

www.speakpub.com

Dying To Be Straight! Too
Michael D. Beckford

ISBN-10: 0-9824189-8-1
ISBN-13: 978-0-9824189-8-7
LCCN: 2013915914

SPEAKPUBLISHING BOOKS EDITION
Attention: Schools, Churches, Corporations and Non-Profit Businesses. SPEAKPUBLISHING books are available at quantity discounts with bulk purchase for educational, business, church or sales promotional use. For information please send an email to *speakpubone@gmail.com* with subject: Bulk ordering, or call 407-470-4462. *Dying To Be Straight! Series Book Two*

Edited By: Harriet Wilson (vip_editing@yahoo.com)
Cover Photograph by: Ashley Williams (astarling@gmail.com)
Cover Design by: Wilken Tisdale III (wilken.tisdale@gmail.com)
Special Thanks To Book Cover Model: Tiffany Minter
First Paperback Edition September 2013
Charlotte, NC

Visit our website at
www.speakpub.com

Dedication

This has truly been a journey for me in my publishing endeavors. This is book seven, and seven is the number of completion. So—I dedicate this book to God above all and to my loyal readers. Thank you, every last one of you who have supported my work as I have continued to mature in my writing and give you, the reader, better stories.

We all have our struggles, no matter what it is, this book just so happens to be a fictional account of Alexis Carter's story. Hope you enjoy. God bless you always.

"The Craving for a woman is like the lighting of a good smoke, her presence is intoxicating."
-Alexis Carter

Prologue: Club S

*A*fter *the first two seconds of meeting a guy, I wish I had never met him. Life on the streets was dirty, but it didn't get dirtier than a pimp. Yes, I said pimp. The very nature of a disgusting thing, which I simply can't imagine dating ever again. So, there it goes, my declaration for the separation of my very existence from the male gender. Yes, I am done with the xy chromosome, and I am happy and deeply satisfied with the double x.*

People are out here thinking this is a game. This here ain't no game! This is life, man. This is my life. Time out for wearing skirts, dresses, and tight linens. Now is the time for baggie jeans, slacks, and sometimes balling shorts. I don't have anybody to impress. I impress myself because I gets mine.

My man used to make me out to be his whore on Sunday and a video vixen for the world on Monday. Yeah, that's right. We made movies, too. Some may say that I was just as much of a dog as he was because I did enjoy the sex. Nevertheless, it wasn't about that.

She looked down; scars from relationships past had her mind bouncing faster than the music that was being played in the club. Her heart never seemed to forgive itself. The malice she felt for her ex was as sharp as a double-edged sword.

The dullness in her figure spoke volumes towards her discontent. Normally, when she was in a room full of women. She was barely able to pour ice on her hormones quick enough. But that particular

Saturday night at Club Sodom was a little bit different for Alexis Carter.

It wasn't about the sex at all. It was about all the hell he put me through and got away with. He was only a man of his word when it came down to seeing me at night. "That Devil!"

Her faint screams were barely recognizable over the booming music. She posted her tiny hips up against the wall. Then, a small tear formed, and another released like hot chocolate on a cold winter's day. But the only thing that was cold about Alexis was her heart.

One by one, each tear represented a specific hurt. Each tear released a particular weight. But her tears went unnoticed. Her tears were like the backdrop of a stage play, they seemed to have written their lines for the rehearsal to the destruction of her life.

With the deep absence of light in the club, besides being at the bar, no one was able to see a thing. Visions of hatred had formed as her tears continued to release memories of sorrow and pain. She lusted after hate for which she harbored against a man who she believed would never care about her again.

Everything he said was based on broken promises. The dude filled my head up with illusions with his sweet talk and seductive touch. He had me believing that I would live the life of a Hollywood star. He blew my head up with dreams that my name would be on 'The Walk of Fame' and a house in Beverly Hills.

We were Hollywood all right. And I did become a star, just not by my will. He released the movies of him and me in our most intimate and passionate moments all over the Internet. It gave me an incredibly bad image. To add insult to the injury, I had to find out about the whole thing being on the Internet from some pervert pastor.

Seriously, what was a pastor doing looking at that amateur porn site that my ex posted me on? I was devastated. Then, word had got around to my friends and that's when I was practically labeled as a no good whore. This label of being a no-good whore seemed to have stuck with me by both men and women since that video had caught fire on the Internet. And contrary to popular belief, just because a person may delete something from a certain page on the Internet doesn't mean that it's truly been deleted.

With the Internet, nothing is deleted and everything is fair game. I sent an email to the host of that amateur porn site after finding out about it. They took it down, but to my amazement, that filth showed up somewhere else. Not only did it show up somewhere else, but also somebody decided to narrate it, as if the sights and sounds of animalistic pleasure weren't enough narration to begin with.

Honestly, I don't know who I am anymore. Every day, I seem to lose one more piece of my soul, and I lose that much more control of myself. People around here be looking at me as if they know me. They judge me as if they know what I've been through.

Her tears had subsided, her loose baggy jeans felt much lighter as she forced herself to move halfheartedly with the music while she loosened up the pin holding her long Pocahontas like black hair. Alexis was often complimented for the richness and solid black texture of her hair, aside from her voluntary minor male like outer appearance; she kept herself well-groomed.

Some people even hate on me because I lust after the flesh of other women and my pent-up desires crave the silky-smooth bottom that was sculptured by the heavens for me to grab and hold on to. Unlike a sculpture, these desires are very real, and I can't help the way that I feel for a nice femme or maybe even a butch, too. Apparently, in this world, these types of desires make me different, maybe even less than a woman.

Pastors on the social networks have lied on me because I haven't been in their line for repentance. One pastor posted on my Facebook page that I was a child born for hell. When I saw that outrageous post and fifty people liked his comment, I shed enough tears that night to fill a small pond. First, what was he doing looking at my videos, and secondly, I thought that pastors were to encourage, not discourage people to seek after God. People like him can go to the bottomless pit and have my fried catfish sandwich ready for me when I get there. I don't even think that the gates of hell are wide enough to fit all the backsliding, trifling, money hungry, sex-crazed pastors that profess to be so— righteous in the eye of the public.

And my mother. Alexis looked on at the bypassing women; she licked her lips in the process, she hoped she could find an easy prey in the cover of darkness. *My mother, oh no, I don't even want to talk about my mother; my mother was a little loose back in her younger days. Let's just say that my mother specialized in lying on her back to pay the bills. Now she acts as if she doesn't even know me at times. Why? Because my mother found God and that's when she began to relish in her religious spirit. She hardly wants anything to do with me because of the choices I have made in my life.*

She acts like she's Miss Goody Two Shoes. She tried to act like she ain't never did something. Shoot, I heard that my mother was looser than two dogs in heat. I just feel like she needs to be more transparent with people, acting like she's such a holy roller. I know her dirty little secrets anyway.

No more lying, no more crying, no more creeping, no more sneaking. The truth, well— let's just say that the truth must be told. And if it's not apparent enough, the truth is this; I, Alexis Carter, am a fully converted lesbian.

She bowed her head, licked her lips, and moved with the rhythm of the music once more.

*****

Pain has been the name of my game ever since the college thing. My life had never been the same. Rats and roaches from back at the crib couldn't have prepared me for this because the people around these parts seem to be dirtier than the dirtiest, grimiest rodent. People are constantly judging me, trying to find a way to put me down. They try to make me feel like a fool, so what if I want to put my arms around my home girl. I got swag, and half of the dudes I run cross hate on my swag because I am pulling more girls

*than them. Just because celebrities like Ellen and Anderson
are out, doesn't mean that I don't get weird stares when I
show my affection in the open.*

Ooh… *look at that honey right there,* "Yeah you
swing those hips, dark chocolate. Come here and let
me put some caramel on it." *That's just for giggles, she
probably can't even hear a sister girl.*

Ooh… *I discovered me a white girl. I love me some
white girls, they form the best partnerships. She's a blonde.
I definitely need to grow some and gone on over there and
talk to her stilettos wearing, chest peculating, lips like
Kool-Aid of a woman. Besides my evident attraction to
white women, I can't help but see it as an added plus. The
majority of them have good money, good credit, good family
history, and well, everything else takes care of itself.*

*Tonight I am on a highly paid woman alert; I rolled
up in Club S by myself, and I'd be crazy to be leaving the
same way I came, so I am doing a full-blown scouting
report. Unlike those punks down the street at Club G, we
don't do any cross-dressing here at Club S.*

*Sodom is the exclusive club in Tallahassee for
women only. Everyone is very discreet, and according to
the many times that I've been here, you're bound to hook-
up with a chick at least, seventy percent of the time that
you come. That's a good statistic. They can do whatever
they like at Gomorrah; we ladies don't have time for the
drama I hear going on at Club G. Apparently the guys at
Club G aren't good at being discreet.*

*I heard that the guys who are on the DL be giving
the boys who are fully out a hard time. There ain't nothing
more amusing than to see two punks fighting, and believe*

me, them boys be fighting worse than chicks, every other week I'd see one of their fights posted up on that world star website.

Girls around here be getting their haircut bald, and they still don't look like dudes, at least, not to me. She shook her head in laughter, as she thought about the many transformations she'd seen in just a few short weeks of attendance at the club. *I don't see the point in cutting my hair, unless I'm about to register for the military; I love to rock my long luscious hair. And the weave business is a little short without me because I rock all natural.*

"Oh my God, Oh my God." *There goes another fine white girl. She thick too. Maybe I should go talk to her, see if I could get that credit card number up off her, and maybe a few more digits while I'm at it. The girl looks like she has a bar tab for six people.*

Alexis lightly scurried her way over to the bar. All sense of humiliation, fear, and depression long left her. Her confidence level was a ten out of ten.

I might as well, make good use of my time here at Club S. It usually gets real live round here at about one in the morning, it's twelve thirty now, so it's time for me to go for the kill shot. She leaned over the bar; she sneaked over and seated herself next to the girl. Her stealth mode worked, she went unnoticed at first glance.

Hollering at a guy and trying to holler at a girl is very different. That's what I be trying to tell these dudes that just blatantly hate on me. Now, if the girl is a hardcore lesbian chick that typically cuts her hair low and is very aggressive, then she's a butch, and hollering at a butch is like hollering at a guy. But if the chick is more girly, a natural acting chick, then she's a femme. There are no laws that say that femme's and femme's can't be together or two butches either. I consider myself a cross between a butch and a femme.

I am a tougher female to figure out because I wouldn't dare cut my hair down like a butch, but I can be very aggressive while also retaining some of my basic feminine qualities.

This is the way I usually like to handle it, "Hey girlfriend, can you imagine anybody better sitting next to you because I can make a million dollars pleased to see you." *I said to the white girl, whom I will call chick number one for now, til' I get her name.*

"No, no one else is coming," chick number one quickly glanced to her left, and then she just as briskly went back to her shots.

"Oh okay, so you don't mind if I sit here next to you." *I'm trying to smooch the girl. So far, it doesn't seem as if it's working, maybe this chick has had a bad day, but she won't even look at me while I'm talking. She can't be straight, straight girls don't come to lesbian clubs. What's her deal?*

"No, I don't mind you sitting here at all," *her head jerked back as she continued to rack up the liquor. It must have been a tough day for this dime piece.*

"I actually came here by myself and am happy to have someone to talk to now. You know a fine woman is hard to find."

She threw me a wink. That's just the confirmation I needed, she's not straight, and she's open for business.

"So what's your name," I asked chick number one, barely hearing her response over J. Lo's new track blazing over the sound system.

After asking me to repeat myself three frustrating times, she finally said, "My name is Karen."

Karen and I shared a few laughs, and even talked a little about our lives. I don't believe she would have shared the stuff that she shared with me on just the first time meeting her if it wasn't for the liquor. We had some similarities in our struggles. Everybody has traumatic issues these days. I hope she wouldn't have an issue with me swiping her credit card numbers; I'm dying for me a new purse. All I need is a few prolific words, and then I'll be at her place of residence before the night is over.

Some girls say that I could be a dog, too aggressive and pushy. I'm nowhere near what some of these girls would do in this club just to score one for the night. I have seen chicks slipping pills in girls' drinks without their permission. I thought that those extremes were exclusive to guys, I guess not; at least, at Club S it happens all the time.

I ain't ever slipped one in a girl's drank, if she doesn't want to go home with me, then fine. I'll take one for the team and keep it moving. I'm too fine to be stressing over no chick. As my homeboy, Skip Blue likes to say, "There are way too many fish in the sea to get caught up slippin, pimpin." *My homeboy is so— hilarious. That dude is the very definition of straight, he's smooth and, oh yeah, very attractive. If I weren't as fascinated about women as I've become, I'd probably try him out for loose change. Otherwise, I'm sticking to what I know, and what I know is sitting right next to me, all alone, ready for me to ask her out.*

"So Karen, you got other plans for tonight, you know the night is still young, if you take down one more shot, girl, you'll be throwing up all over the club." Alexis paused. "Hey, why don't we go get some fresh air, talk about our problems, and you know, go from there?"

"Yeah, that sounds fun; I need to get out of here. Hey, what's your name?"

"I'm Alexis, but my friends call me Lexi. You can call me Lexi." She licked her lips with more desperation; she was excited about the promise of a good time for a few hours. A time when God's laws are broken, a moment which passion often overrides the guilt, Alexis was ready to sin again.

"Okay Lexi, where do you want to go first?" Karen slipped the bartender her card and left a cash tip on the table.

"Well… um… I was thinking my place. I have a nice 'lil' apartment with a balcony with the capitol building in view. I figured we can order out some wings or something." *I hope she takes the bait; the surge of feelings below my waist can't stand it anymore. I'm ready to have some fun.*

"Alright that's fine with me; at least, we don't have to pay a cover charge." Karen laughed.

Either this girl is that ditsy, or my game is just hot. It doesn't even matter now; I got her confirmation, now it's just time to get to second base because when I do, I know I'm scoring a home run.

"You ready." Karen asked a little light on her feet, a little tipsy too.

"Yeah, I'm ready. Let's go."

Ready set here I go, on to the new life in which I know. Lusting after women like a woman to a man, my life is indignant of God's plan. I love this life too much to turn back now, can't a man do what a woman can, her lips, her breast, her tender sweet touch, oh the thought of her all over me is just too much. I used to like that feeling. That touch of a man, but my ex-boyfriend ruined my opinion of all men. I'm dying to be straight, too; at least, that's what I tell myself. But my actions say another thing, maybe one day I will truly find myself. For now, Karen is the sheep and I am the wolf. I will devour her because my hormones have spoken.

Welcome to Club S, it's always a girls' night out here.

Part 1

"Because of this, God gave them over to shameful lusts. Even their women exchanged natural relations for unnatural ones. In the same way, the men also abandoned natural relations with women and were inflamed with lust for one another. Men committed indecent acts with other men, and received in themselves the due penalty for their perversion."

-Romans 1:26-27

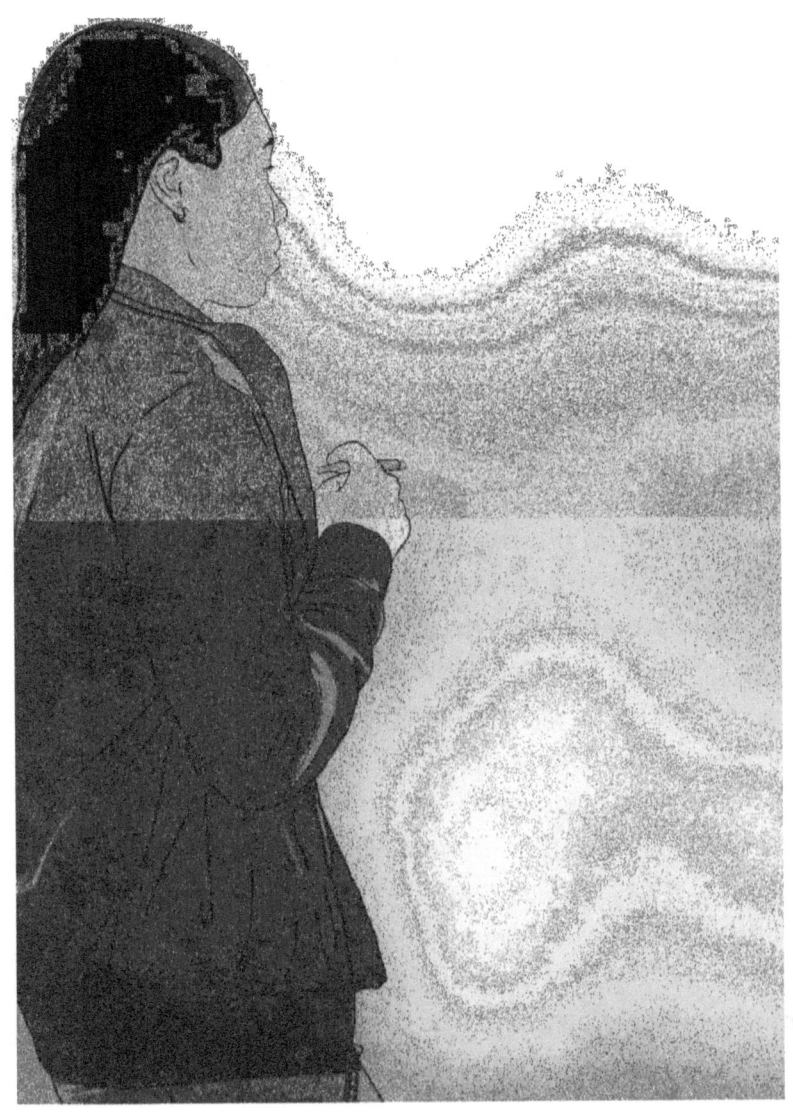

What is it worth?

I remember back in the day when mama used to braid my hair. That's when she was skating between loving God and loving men. She didn't think that my sisters and I woke up to the sounds of love making at two in the morning, and if she really liked the guy, she'd let him stay til' six, an hour before we had to get ready to leave for school. Mama always tried to cover up her dirt, but my sisters, Sabrina and Brandy, noticed. We knew everything. My mother had about five different men coming in or out, one way or the other, while I was only seven. She never introduced us to any of the men. I never knew why at the moment. I always wondered if one of those men could be our daddy. Mama just wanted a quickie, and she was afraid of what her double lifestyle could do to us.

Of course, at such an early age, I didn't understand much. I was still playing with Barbie dolls, and boys always smelled bad to me. I didn't fully understand at the time that mama was a freak and running a business in her bedroom, specifically on the mattress.

Mama always loved to sing, if she wasn't such a heathen when I was seven, she could have been one of the leading voices in somebody's choir. Not like there ain't no heathens in the choir, but mama had too many late-night flings that would have caused her to be late for early-morning service. Lord knows, the only early-morning service she was getting, was the penetration from some random guys protruding penis elevated through her vaginal walls.

Mama was a neat freak of sorts, house always had to be swept and mopped on a daily basis. Bathroom had to be cleaned two times a day, and nobody was going to bed unless the kitchen was 'Mr. Clean' type clean. She spared no time when it came down to laying that rod down on my two sisters and me if the house wasn't straight. At least, Proverbs 13:24 was a Scripture my mother didn't mind obeying when it came down to keeping our butts in line. Somebody should have been keeping her in line on Exodus 20:14 because she slept with a many of married men.

I had some good times growing up. I just was a girl who loved school, enjoyed playing outside, and had fun in Sunday school, whenever mama made up her mind for us to go to church.

We were the occasional pew dwellers. We knew about God, but I'm not sure if he knew us. Church for me back then was just another form of social escape; I'd usually chat with some of my girlfriends from school and laugh at the immature boys in attendance. Of course, living in Miami always brought on a daily forecast of hot, so we'd chase the ice-cream man down after church to get some quarter popsicles and fifty-cent carton juice. Life was fun at that age; I still had my innocence, although my sisters and I were constantly exposed to my mother's forays. I was at an age of learning many things and asking a million questions of course.

I loved watching 'The Jefferson's 'at the tender age of eleven, the age when my mother started introducing us to her men. She started slowing down a bit, wasn't straddling the fence as hard, but when she was stressed, which we knew when she was stressed, there usually was a mini-band being directed in her room. Subsequently, my sisters and I used to sneak to her door to hear it, whatever man she was with was usually the drum major, and she was the drum. We would hear a masterpiece of 'Ooohs... And ahhs...' being performed as the headboards hit the wall and the springs from the bed often added that additional note from the tambourine section.

Unfortunately, the consequence of our mother's forays was our first introduction to men; this is what we believed men were meant for. Men were made in the spitting image of a male dog we saw on the street, taking advantage of a female dog in heat and off to the next dog he could meet.

The images of mama being held captive in her bed were so real to me. Although I knew that it was all consensual, my mind raced with the thoughts of sex and the type of bondage that was recently made popular by that, "Fifty Shades of Grey" book. I was young, and that's what life was like when I looked around our neighborhood, women with children and no man. Yes, there were the casual thugs walking around the neighborhood with pants sunk lower than my dress, but there weren't the visual men I had seen on television like The Jefferson's and The Cosby's. So I figured, that maybe, just maybe, our neighborhood in Miami Carol City was just special. Maybe our men went off to the military and to college with the promises of coming back home. But after eleven years of time spent on this earth, my daddy never came. He never came back, so there I was confused.

I was confused because here I was watching television, but it wasn't what was going on in the real *world. At eleven years old, girls were having their period and lending themselves to the highest bidder. Babies were having babies in a sense, while having kids out of wedlock was the order of the day. This was the world that I saw, women struggling, waiting on their next government check. Food Stamps ran out the same day they were received. There were no men of honor or men of standards in our community. No Jesse Jackson or Al Sharpton to save us, the hood was wild and we knew it. Drug dealers and pimps were our role models; they were the voice of our hood, maybe even our version of Bill Cosby and George Jefferson. This was the world I knew, a world better known to most outsiders as **the projects**.*

It wasn't til' I was fourteen when I put myself on the auction block, I could no longer stand the pent-up rage for sex screaming inside me. It's almost as if when my period first came on, there was a whole new programming of my DNA, boys were no longer the nemesis in my mind. It was as if I took a pill like Neo in the Matrix and saw men for who they really were. Not just dogs, but pleasure monkeys, and I knew that with the right guy knowing exactly what to do, then the pleasure I had anticipated would be so right and yet so wrong.

I wanted to discover what my older sister, Sabrina, experienced, I wanted to sing the songs of passion like mama did. I wanted to be kept. I wanted to be held. I wanted a guy to satisfy all my needs, and at the age of fourteen, I wanted a guy so bad. I was like a female dog in heat, and at the time it didn't matter to me if the guy had other girls he had to take care of, as long as he took care of me, I felt that I'd be alright.

Fresh Meat

*I*t was the fall of 2003; I was bringing in the new school year swagged out. Mama had made some extra money in overtime and bought each of my sisters and me fifteen brand new outfits. I swear that had to be the most she'd ever spent on us three girls. It had to have been like seven hundred dollars on clothes alone, and she dropped another three-fifty on shoes. Being the middle child and all, I always felt like the black sheep, seemed like mama always paid more attention to Brandy, the youngest, who was in elementary school at the time and my older sister Sabrina, who was moving into her junior year in high school. I'm the one that encouraged mama to get the fits; Brandy didn't even need that many outfits because she had to wear a uniform. But as mama would always say, "What I do for one child, I will have to do for the other."

Dressed and ready to impress, I was fresh meat on the campus of Miami Carol City, home of the mighty Chiefs, around those parts they just called it Carol City, the school on N. W. 187th Street. Being fresh meat and wearing fabulous digs, I was an instant target for sex hungry males, to some girls they might have took to defense, for me, well, let's just say that I was right where I wanted to be. I loved the attention they gave me, if they weren't looking at me, then something had to be wrong with them. At fourteen years old, I had curves like my mother, fully developed breasts like my sister Sabrina and a flat chiseled stomach like my sister Brandy. Oh, I had the best of three worlds; I guess being a middle child did have a few perks.

I even loved the way my mother looked at me in the face as she clutched my chin and twisted me east and west questioning if I was involved in sexual activities. My fall semester I wasn't. I was too busy being the pretty girl, and loved being a tease. There were certain stimuli I felt when I teased a guy, I always eyed him carefully paying close attention to his reaction and his sweet melodies he spoke to me to try to get me in bed. Besides fall semester, I also was grinding on my schoolwork. I loved school and high school at the time was new to me, so I had to make sure my grades were right before I was all booed up.

My spring semester was a snail's paced different from my fall semester. Springtime brings spring flowers, spring showers and…. It was mating season for me. My grades were doing well, and I decided to finally take the plunge, dive in headfirst, and select the premier guy who seemed to make all the trouble around school.

I didn't want an athlete because I figured they probably had an STD. But I did want a bad boy, a guy who still had the chiseled abs, plump biceps and an impression I could see below the waste. My home girls and I always giggled about how important it was to be with a guy who stretched across the ruler, as if his thing was running the marathon or something. Even though I was still a virgin at the beginning of my spring semester, I had seen enough dirty magazines, websites and sex text to know the difference between a man that stretched across the ruler, and one that was barely visible to the naked eye. So— I really kind of wanted an athlete, but without the athlete baggage.

So, my first boo was Ricky. Ricky Wilder was his name. That boy was a six feet two-hundred and five-pound monster. He was a junior at the time; with dreads as long as my hair and four distinguishing gold teeth in his mouth, he was everything I wanted. He was one of the guys stalking me down since the fall semester. I knew he knew I was a virgin, for one, because I didn't give it up that easy, and two, it's like people around there could smell if you're sexually active. I smelt of purity, wholeness, a young woman with grown woman feelings, and an appetite for sex that was held back for too long. I needed Ricky to quench my thirst, be the master of my domain, and make me feel good about what everyone in my school and neighborhood was talking about and doing. I wanted to be pleased between the sheets, on top of the sheets, and even under the bed if he was down for it.

Ricky Wilder was the bad boy I was looking for. He came to school as he pleased, got into fights and won, and as an eleventh grader, he had a swagged out brand new black 2003 Dodge Charger. One of his rims cost more than my two sisters and my outfits alone. The boy was constipated with money; he had everything I thought I needed at the time. Although he acted like a thug with his lil' homies in public, privately he was a really nice guy.

*****

"What up, chick. What it is you be up to today?" Ricky Wilder licked his lips and smiled at a precariously over enthusiastic Alexis. He pulled out his swagger card, and he decided to run another line on her that one fateful high school day. "Yo chick. Let's chill in my hooptie, girl, let's get blowed."

"Boy you ain't got no hooptie, what you talking about. And you know I don't smoke, right." She lightly nudged him in his rib cage.

"Girl, why you got to nudge me in my ribs in front of all these people in this courtyard? And yes, for the sixth time, I know you say you don't smoke, but how bout the last time I was rolling up one I saw you was looking like you was feigning for a puff." He tightened his grip around her waist.

"Boy, you so stupid. I wasn't looking at you for a blunt. I was trying to give you a signal to stop, and the smoke started getting to me. Y'all little boys don't ever understand a female's intuitions. Y'all make all your decisions with one head and assume that's the law of the day." She smirked, and then moved slowly an inch or two in his face to show that she was serious.

He responded with laughter, clearly he wasn't expecting her to be in the 'Don't Touch Zone' usually when someone rolled up in his face a fight was quickly to ensue. That's one of the benefits Alexis enjoyed by being his girlfriend. She could be in his face all she wanted, and she loved and craved that type of power.

"Girl, you know that you want to tap that blunt."

That ain't the only thing that I want him to tap. She smiled. "Wait a minute, are we still talking about the same thing?" She quizzed him.

"What do you mean?" He asked with a look of confusion stretched across his perfectly shaped dark chocolate-coated circle.

She felt bad. She knew she had to come up with a quick exit strategy, or as most people properly phrased it as *a lie*. "Oh, I just kind of thought that you were talking about my goodies when you were talking about hitting that blunt," she replied. Because of her pent-up feelings for him, she decided that honesty superseded whatever lie she could have made up.

"Girl, I gets plenty of chicks hocking my mantle, and none of the females I done been with had a complaint, matter of fact, chicks still trying to bed ride with me. I have to brush them off now since me and you done got hooked up." He looked away, he knew that part of his story was a lie. He was with one of his faithful flings the other night.

Lashanda was one of Ricky's on and off again *jump off chicks*, but the fact that she always was submissive to his every beckoning call no matter how much she hated him, was what made her faithful to him in spite of all the women she had witnessed Ricky go through like a water sport.

Alexis nodded her head. "Sure, tell me anything Ricky. Tell me anything. I know you still got chicks on speed dial that's just waiting to devour you. We only been dating for like two weeks, and I ain't put out like your other project chicks probably did for you after one day. So I got you nervous now, you wondering if I'm gone let go my guard and let down my heart."

She continued her discussion with much vigor and satisfaction. "You want you a virgin girl, cause it's probably something you ain't get to experience head first in the hood. Girls are so trifling round here. I had seen this twelve-year-old girl run out this dude house that had to been at least, twenty-five. The girl barely understood her body, but there she was giving it away for free."

At least, mama knew how to get paid for her services. Alexis became immediately aggravated and consumed with the thoughts of her own level of inexperience in the area of sex.

"Just to let you know, I ain't no regular project hoe. I ain't giving my stuff to anybody, but if the right guy takes me off my feet, loves me, and is committed to me, then maybe, just maybe that guy will find out what's buried beneath my jeans."

Breathless, Ricky quickly tried to find a comeback; finally, he had a real challenger, a woman who wasn't just willing to dangle the thread of her panties, but one willing to challenge him to be a *do right man*, or so he thought.

I got him right where I want him, he looks like he really fell for that bull, I want the same thing them hoochie mamas want, I'm just gone make him work for it a little bit longer. Shoot, why can't a chick have fun, too, without being labeled a hoe? Stay grounded Alexis. Stay grounded. Alexis told herself. *This brother right here looks good to me. I got me a fine piece of specimen.*

Alexis was so caught up in her mid moment fantasies. She didn't even hear when Ricky nudged for her attention.

"Lexi, did you hear me?" he asked her again, frustrated and sweaty.

"Yeah, yeah, I heard you boo." She lied. All she heard were here hormones knocking on hell's door. Passions and desires she suppressed made their way back in her presence.

He knew she was lying. "Yeah, so what did I say?"

She quickly wanted to defend herself, her jaws dropped from his liar comment. There was only one way out to defend her peace and honor, so she played Russian roulette with her words, she knew she only had one bullet to give. "I don't remember what you said, but I heard you, and don't call me no liar, little boy. You hurt my feelings." She balled up and pushed herself away from a shocked and bewildered Ricky. She turned away with a devilish smirk and knew that she got her one shot in on Ricky; she believed that she won.

Ricky caught on to her game, he backed up a bit and he, too, pulled the trigger. "Oh no, you didn't trick, you trying to turn this around on me. I done peeped out your game. It's a game of cat and mouse. This ain't Disney chick. Do I look like goofy to you?" He pulled back his rant. It gave them both the comic relief they needed. And just as the clock hit twelve and they were turning in their silver slippers, they both rolled in laughter; onlookers gawked at the very site of their sudden emotional outburst.

I think I'm going to love this boy; he's cute when he's angry, and he makes me laugh.

"So— what did you say Ricky, I really didn't hear you?" She leaned over and placed one finger after the other in the palm of his hand. She affectionately placed her face back in the 'Don't Touch Zone' not for a fight, but to perhaps wrestle him for a kiss. A kiss she hoped would be her first with him.

He ignored her sudden lust for him, he responded to her question. "Well, it's too late now, don't worry about it." He blew her off.

"I got to get to class, Mrs. Smith warned me that the next time I'm late for her class cuz, then that's like an automatic detention. We can talk about it after school or something." He smiled, and then flirtatiously winked at her.

Her hope for a kiss was accelerated again, as every part of her body was praising the good news, her flesh wanted to be touched, it wanted to be satisfied. She leaned in on him again, that time close enough to hear him breathing.

A little bit of excitement was also triggered under his clothing, but because he did not want to seem weak and not having a grain of self-control, he lightly pushed back and said, "I got to get to class Lexi."

And just like that, he walked away and left her hot and heavy with emotions. She didn't know whether to grab his backpack, turn him around and slap him or grab the corner of his hips, turn him around, and strike a deep penetrating kiss like a rattlesnake going in on its prey. And just as her crazy thoughts were about to become actions, the bell rang again and Ricky was already fifteen feet ahead of her.

"Man, this dude is gone drive me crazy. I'll be lucky to keep my v-card for the next three weeks than the original three months I originally planned to test him out on." She whispered under her breath as she packed up her things for class, a class in which if she didn't hurry to be there in the allotted forty-five seconds, she would have been marked late like her older sister's menstrual cycle.

Taken

I couldn't have been more wrong with my thoughts
about men at the tender age of fourteen, although I
knew that men were dogs, cheats, and totally after the
cookies. I couldn't have been more wrong in my perception
of men, not only did I find out that men were everything
negative that I could have ever imagined, but they were the
thugs, the playas and the pimps that haunted my worst
nightmares. They were nasty, scheming and a low down
dirty shame. Men got games, and unless you are ready to
play the game of monopoly with them, your heart will truly
go bankrupt.

*Truth be told, I didn't care that a man knew how to
be a man, but what messed me up was the fact that I fell in
love with a male whore. Yes, I said it, Ricky Wilder, the
guy of my dreams was more than an occasional cheat, and
he was the very picture pasted in the dictionary, glued in
on the hearts of women as a male whore. To make it so bad,
my boo loved his status. I hated it.*

"What up Lexi, what the biznesss is? I hope
you like the flowers I laid round your porch." He
looked on into her desert brown eyes, he licked his
lips and peeked at her curves. Truly obsessed at her
waistline, he slowly pulled her into him as he dabbed
a kiss on her left cheek.

He hoped the neighbors weren't watching
them on her front porch, Alexis quickly pushed him
away, her mother wasn't scheduled to be home for an
hour and her two sisters were off to the corner store

to get chocolate chip cookies and jungle juice. Three months had passed and Alexis had continued to keep herself pure, at least, in the terms of vaginal intercourse, her willingness to experiment with other sexual innuendos had not been met with the same act of self-control. She gave in to the pressures of oral sex and dry humping (a teenager's rite of passage in the world of underage premarital sex) within the first month of their relationship.

So, for the two love birds with a workaholic mother gone, two sisters at the store, and nosey neighbors who didn't seem to care, this was the perfect setup for two non-adults to partake in adult-like activities.

"Ricky, you know I'm on my period right now. Besides, I— can't— you— know go all the way with you." She looked down, felt ashamed about the pattern of her period and her desire to truly go all the way.

I've done just about everything in the book, why don't I go all the way? Why am I still pretending to hold out on my virginity as if this is still some game? Grandma always said that legs closed are allowing the super power in you to take charge as a woman. Legs open, well, grandma said that legs open leaves you with a belly open wide.

"Lexi, hello, I'm still here." Ricky looked at her as if he was confused at her constant staring into space. His emotions were pent-up, and the desire to release the seeds of his image into another innocent girl, had him all but ready to explode. But just as always, he was cool, calm, and in disguise like the jaws of an alligator hidden, camouflaged and ready to take first bite. Besides, in his mind, he still had a couple of honeys on his VIP list. These were the women he gave special treatment when they called, these were also the women that paid him to be with them.

Some of the women ranged from sixteen upwards to thirty, although most of the thirty-year old women he messed with were normally newly divorced and wanted a young fling like Ricky Wilder to bring back the spark in their bedroom.

The older women ranged in a variety of respectable professions, some were doctors, lawyers, and even teachers. They paid top dollar for him to be their escort for just one night.

"Alright Lexi, what do you want to do? I'm all ears." He loosened up his grip a bit.

She smiled. "Well, I just kind of want to chill for a bit. I'm hungry." She exhaled, she abandoned her thoughts about sex, she hoped that Ricky would understand her plea to just chill.

With a little hint of disappointment, his lips shifted down a bit, and then he smiled for a brief second and displayed each row of his pearly whites. "Yeah, I'm cool with that, let's go inside."

Dang man, this chick will keep a brutha dry if it wasn't for the other skeezers I got lined up.

After a few minutes of back and forth conversation on the porch, they finally entered her three-bedroom apartment. Ricky smelt the fragrance of seduction which pulsated from the dark caramel, round bottom skin of Alexis.

She could feel his eyes on her butt and with one quick motion she turned around. "Boy what you looking at?" She asked. He jumped, he was knocked out of his daze of affection and lust; he was hungry, and he was ready to devour every part of her.

Ricky paused for a moment, then with a deep exhale from his wide nostrils, he said, "Girl, you crazy, you know how bad I want to tap that." A surge of excitement lingered below his waist and with another heavy breath. "What are we doing here in the hallway, let's go to your room?"

Her eyebrows twitched sideways at his comment, she wanted to scream and tell him how bad she wanted him, too. "And do what Ricky? What are we going to do in my room?" She asked a rhetorical question, she knew that with her feminine issues of blood that came once a month, she couldn't do anything but hold his hand or cuddle him. But knowing Ricky, she knew that more was on his mind than a little cuddling. She knew that he wanted her on her knees to perform the unmentionable activities of their limbs.

She tried to play it safe and pretend that everything was going to be good and Ricky would really be satisfied with just cuddling. But to her preconceived notions after entering into her room, she couldn't have been so wrong and so right at the same time. Ricky Wilder wanted her to perform other adult activities, similar to what they had done at least five

times before. But never was she on her menstrual
during any of those times. A level of discomfort filled
her mind. She lightly pushed away from Ricky, and
she looked at the time and thought about her sisters
and mother's return. Her menstrual always had made
her feel dirty, and the thought of performing oral sex
just added insult to injury to an already
uncomfortable recurring cycle.

"Ricky, I think it's time for you to go. My
peoples will be here any minute now, and my mother
would kill me if she saw me in the room with you like
this. What am I thinking? I could get in a lot of
trouble Negro." She waited patiently for a response as
she laid back on her bed, she was ready to pull the
switch on their few minutes together. She also used
the impending presence of her mother and sisters as a
tool for Ricky to leave, so she wouldn't have to bare
the temptation that was sure to increase by the
second.

"Don't worry about them, girl, I got your back,"
he replied, and smiled with a confident wink.

There he goes again, thinking with the other head.
"Well, do you have my front, cuz my mother doesn't
have a problem with swiping that belt across my
breast!"

Ricky looked at her real quick. He didn't know
how to respond to her question, he slowly bent down
to kiss her on the lips, and she turned away. He
pulled his body to her left side. She turned the other
way, then he tried to kiss her once more. He still
missed the target.

"Lexi, what's up? You don't even want to kiss me now." He said with a childish rage, he showed the makeup of his seventeen years on the earth.

Many of his other female flings loved to say that he was a grown man trapped in a young man's body. That mode of thinking couldn't be more untrue, the Ricky Wilder that went home at night was a young man in a young man's body. He may have matured in areas where other males his age were behind sexually, but his mind was still ravished by video games, crazy locker room conversations, and his alter ego thug persona on Myspace.com while MySpace was near its peak of popularity.

Ricky still had to answer to his young thirty-six year old mother of three, he, being the oldest of the three boys. He surely wasn't the type of role model that most parents would like for their children to look up to, but he was the only role model his two younger brothers had, each with different daddies. As the story goes in the projects, daddy was never anywhere to be around in his home either; he grew up in the projects a mile away from Alexis. Ricky's role models, unfortunately, were the drug dealers, thugs, and pimps. Although those so-called role models of his chose to keep a low profile, everyone in the neighborhood knew who they were.

"It's not a matter of me not wanting to kiss you; I just don't like—um— I don't feel comfortable about this right now. I don't know how to explain it. I mean I want you bad, boy, believe me when I say that to you, but being on my period and trying to do other things just don't really work for me. I hope you can understand that, Ricky. And I am for real about what I said; my mother will be here any minute now. Brenda doesn't play her radio when it comes down to boys being in the house."

"But I thought you said that she was cool." He looked at her with grave disappointment.

Oh my God this chick is bout to drive me insane. That's what I like about them grown women, I don't have to sneak around and be on the lookout for their mamas. They pay me well, and they already know what they want and what I'm coming there to do. I don't even know why I waste my time with these young tricks any more. It's just too much work to get a few minutes release.

"Yeah, she's cool with us being on the front porch, but not in my room with the door closed and your pants nearly unzipped, with one of my breasts taking a peak of the room."

"Okay, well—cool I get it. I'll go ahead and leave then. We can catch up another time or something. I wouldn't want big bad Brenda to swat me with a belt or something. My mother would normally discover anything she could find to whoop my brothers with it. You know how black women are."

"Yeah I know. My mama will fight my sisters and me. She put the belt away a long time ago. Wait a minute, shhh...did you hear that?" Alexis was instantly frightened by the noise she thought she heard.

"No, I didn't hear anything," he whispered while he zipped up his fly. *This chick has gone crazy.*

"Alexis, we're back," Sabrina announced at the top of her lungs. "Mamma called me on my cell and said that she'll be here in five minutes, where you at girl."

"I heard that." Ricky smiled at his awkward confession. He quickly picked himself off the bed and headed straight for Alexis's room door to exit the house as quickly as he could.

Meanwhile, Alexis had covered herself back up and fixed herself the best way she knew how. She knew that Sabrina wasn't going to tell her mother a thing, but it was Brandy that she was worried about who was known as being the *household snitch.*

"Hey, wait a minute, Ricky, let me check to see where my younger sister at. That brat tells mama everything." She opened her room door and peeked outside. She knew she only had five minutes to spare so she had to put a plan in place as quick as possible. She caught Sabrina's attention, and Sabrina knew instantly what was going on, so she signaled to Alexis that the path was clear, her little sister ran into the bathroom as soon as they entered the house.

Alexis paced back into her room and pulled Ricky outside her door. "Hey, go through the back door, so mama won't see you when she comes."

"Okay."

Alexis heard the bathroom toilet flush and knew she only had fifteen seconds before her sister came out of the bathroom, so she lightly pushed

Ricky forward. She forced him to make his way out of the back door before Brandy opened the bathroom door. She was successful, and just like clockwork, Brenda made her entry through the front door and Brandy exited the bathroom.

Ricky, on the other hand, walked away mumbling and pouting under his breath. He was not happy. He thought about calling up one of his girls on his VIP list, but then again, he knew that there would be some sort of drama with one of them, too. So he pulled a blunt out of his pocket and lit it up. "This world can't handle me, chicks are a dime a dozen, and I'm here to take what's rightfully mine," he declared as he was already half way to his house.

Crash Course

Ricky never sold a dime of weed in his life or any other drug, for that matter, but he'd smoke a bag til' his face turned blue. Ricky Wilder chose to follow more in the footsteps of the pimp he admired growing up, especially since he felt that he, too, was God's gift to women, he loved to see the pretty women that often got out of the limo with the pimp. Ricky even admired the colorful clothing this particular pimp wore on Friday and Saturday, those two nights were what Michael Lewis (the pimp) would call prime time pimping. Those nights brought in massive, exceeding amounts of cash for Michael as he had set his women up on the corners of South Beach and downtown Miami. Rarely did Michael place any of his girls in the projects. When he did demand for one of his girls to be in the projects, it was often because the girl had either tried to cross him with his money, or she thought about quitting the game.

Michael had control of seven girls. All were wrapped around his fingers with the promise of protection and room and board. Of course, he gave them a small percentage of the business they brought in, and with the onslaught of ballas that were constantly in and out of South Beach and downtown for Miami Heat and Hurricane games. Business was always good. Of course, Michael Lewis also had competition, but he knew how to keep the competition at bay.

Michael had a few cops, lawyers, and judges on payroll. Most times he didn't even have to pay, he kept many of the cops, judges, and lawyers happy with his girls, especially on those nights when they and their wives didn't see eye to eye. They would call Michael for a quick fix. Sex is a drug like cocaine, and Michael knew that once he got them hooked on his women, they would rarely ask for cash.

As a little boy, one thing that Ricky was never able come to terms with was why was Michael still living in the projects? At the tender age of eight, he figured he'd creep up to Michael's place to ask him such a bold question. Michael had more money than time on his hands, he introduced *little Ricky* to the pimp game, *little Ricky* was the nickname, which Michael called him at the time. Michael gave him a crash course on the game of pimping at only eight years old.

"You see little Ricky. The game of pimping is like the game of chess. Perception is everything and you got to be thinking about a thousand moves at a time before you make your first move. Listen here now slick, my apartment here in the projects only represents my one move, well, let me break it down for you son. The projects is where I bring some of my girls, this is where I provide them food, room and board and an Ak-47 to protect their little butts. But, oh my, how wrong could you be to believe that this is where I live all the time. For tax purposes, my name is on this apartment and the government thinks I just make ten-thousand dollars a year at my part-time custodial gig. Which I do make the ten-thousand dollars, but you want to know something lil' son? I don't work at no custodial place. I pay this dude a lil over fifteen grand, who happens to be a friend of mine to put me down on his payroll. Like I said, it's for all intensive tax purposes."

Ricky looked around dumbfounded, he never even heard of Uncle Sam. And to his appeasement, he didn't even know what taxes were.

"Now for a young mind like yourself, you're probably thinking that's crazy. But for an older blood like me, it makes perfect sense. See, this pimp business is virtually an all cash business, no paper trail, and in order to stay in the game. It ain't about how much money you make, but about how much money you can keep. And listen to me clearly little Ricky, if you want to keep the IRS off your butt, show them that you make as little money as possible while you stack up your cheddar elsewhere. Little Ricky, I got a four bedroom house on South Beach and one in the Bahamas. Of course, they both under somebody else's name. It ain't hard to get a fake ID and social security numbers, each pawn in the end leads back to me without them even knowing it." He paused and caught his breath; Michael was always was excited about his business affairs.

"And I will tell you one other thing, lil shorty, having girls is like having a franchise. I put up the capital to keep them with a place to stay, and food, and stuff. They put out the goods, and I make back eighty percent off everything they do on every night. It's the perfect transactions of goods and services," he laughed.

"You do the math, lil bro. If a man says he wants whatever for a hundred dollars and I'm getting that eighty off seven girls, that's a quick five-sixty off the top. But here's my last word to you, shorty, don't get in this game unless you ready to go to jail, get killed, or strung out on some substance. I seen many cats end up losing their minds after the girls and the cops done turned on them. This business can be very lucrative and dangerous at the same time."

Ricky shook his head. He tried his best to seem interested. Actually he was interested, but it was just too much information for an eight year old child to take in at one time.

"Also one last thing, as a code of silence, you don't tell nobody what I told you, and if you do get in the game of pimping, make sure you stay out of my territory shorty. You will know where my corners are, believe me, everyone knows by now. Those are my rules; you are free to take your women anywhere else but my turf."

"Alright." Ricky tried to sound hard as best he could as an eight year old in the third grade. He thought he had life all figured out at that age, but he couldn't have been more wrong. Eight years after that conversation with Michael, Michael Lewis was sent to prison for tax evasion and for tampering with a federal judge. He pleaded no contest and received twelve years for his crimes. On paper, he wasn't scheduled to be released til' late 2015.

Michael played his game of chess for years and finally lost. His downfall was the money became too much for him to hide. He had stashes and stashes under the bed and oftentimes brought a stack to the bank when he really had to make a big purchase that didn't accept cash payments. The banks got suspicious of his hefty deposits and tipped off the government. And just like that, he was under the watchful eye of the FBI and special IRS investigators; they followed him and his money trail for two years before making the arrest in the summer of 2003.

Ricky, on the other hand, chose to pimp in a different way; he became the whore and collected all the money, all the while he kept it low key and a steady girlfriend as usual. Alexis didn't know that she was a part of a deeper plot of Ricky Wilder's dreams, he wanted to turn her out and send her to the streets. He was almost ready to franchise himself, and he was in the process of building up all the capital to do it. Yes, he loved sex and wasn't willing to give it up for the world, but there was only one him and plenty of unsuspecting women to be taken.

It was his first crash course in life, and the only life lessons that he was taught by an adult male.

The Flesh is Weak

Ricky Wilder was busy at home drawing up his business plan for his future pimping enterprise. School had let out early, and he was eager to finalize some of the logistics of his project. Even though he was only a thousand dollars short of his capital goal, which he could have easily made in a week, he still had to wait til' he'd turn eighteen to break away from his mother's custody and file as an independent. Caught up and mesmerized by all the money he could potentially make in a year, he was suddenly startled by the heavy knock on his door. But who could it have been. His brothers were still in their middle school classes and his mother didn't get home til' six and it was only two- thirty in the afternoon.

Who in the world is knocking on my room door? I need me a gun to protect myself. I thought I had done locked the front door of the house. Ricky silently feared what was waiting for him outside his room door.

The knock came again, but it was much louder than the previous knock. He sat up in his bed silent for a minute. He hoped that it was a dream, or whoever it was that knocked on his room door, he hoped that they got the hint. Unfortunately, they didn't. They knocked again, and what followed the knock was a shout of his name. "Ricky, open the door fool." It was Alexis; she made her way to his house without informing him in advance. That was a no-no in his book.

Because he didn't want to be marked as exerting suspicious activity, he replied, "Okay, give me a second." He slung his business plans under the bed, her name was boldly written on the map to be one of his future prostitutes, and just as he was about to open the door, he remembered that he had one of his thirty-year old chicks over the previous night. The girl left a trail.

"Oh, no, she left her bra." He mumbled to himself.

"What's going on in there? Ricky, open the door." Alexis grew impatient. She stomped her feet on the floor in anger.

Ricky quickly grabbed the handle to the window and slung the bra outside. "Just one second, baby, my room is a mess."

Just as Alexis pondered to go home or not, Ricky briskly opened the door and let her in. *One of my little brothers are going to get it, leaving the front door open all the time. This ain't the 'Little House on The Prairie', this here is the hood, and leaving the front door open is how cats round here get robbed and shot.*

Alexis looked around suspiciously; she eyed every part of his bed, floor, and closet door.

"You ain't got no other hoochie hiding in the closet do you?" she asked with a slow grin on her face. She knew her man had to be up to more than just cleaning up the room. She quickly leaped for the closet door, and then just to pretend she didn't care, she let go of the door knob. Then, she sat down on the bed next to where Ricky was already seated.

With a sigh of release, he said, "So you don't trust me." He tried to make her feel guilty for her actions.

"I don't trust any Negroes. I don't even trust my own daddy, so how you gone expect me to trust your butt. The only reason I ain't open your closet is because I'm too pretty to fight some hoochie, I just got my nails done, and I ain't bout to break them."

"So, what brings you here unannounced?" Ricky tried to sound as smooth, calm, and collected about it, but really, he harbored anger towards her because she broke rule number one of the man code.

What if I did have some other chick over here and she done caught me in the act? I got to set this girl right and be more careful. Now I see why Michael Lewis had a couple of houses.

"Maybe I decided to come here for what's in your front pocket. You ain't been showing me no love like you used to. What? You done gave up on me since I ain't went all the way with you yet?" She sucked her teeth and waited for a quick response.

He had no response. He knew that she was right, three months had passed, and he'd gotten tired of trying to get her to submit. It was the end of their school summer session, and he was on his way to being a senior, and she was to be a sophomore in high school. He figured he'd come at her with a different approach, especially since he already had a stockpile of women on his waiting list, he figured, *What's one more woman, she'll come around.*

"I don't know, Lexi, it's whatever. I do have feelings for you, I just been real busy with school, keeping my brothers out of trouble, and taking care of my mom. My time just seems to zoom past me. You know what I mean?" He looked back at her, that time she had a quirky look on her face.

"Yeah, I know what you mean." She pulled him closer to her.

"What's up?" He didn't have a clue what she was doing.

She slowly started from the top of her pink button up shirt and directed him to unbutton the rest. He did exactly as he was told. Then, with a look of confusion he asked, "So what you want to do?"

"Shhh…, this is my show, let me run this. Meanwhile, take a loose my bra from the back, remember it has that lil clingy thing, so be careful."

He did exactly as directed; he acted as if it was his first time. After one more metal was loosed, he was blindsided by the firmness of her breast, they formed a perfect circular stratosphere. Mesmerized as if he was a virgin himself, he gazed on to her chest like an explorer to the stars in the olden days.

"Loosen up my belt buckle," she whispered in his ears. He started fast, but she tapped his hands to slow down. As he loosened her belt, he slowly began to pull her blue jeans down, it revealed her rich and youthful high yellow skin. Finally, he took a glimpse of her prime real estate, as her undergarments were the same hot pink as her button up shirt.

"What's next?" he asked like a kid in the candy store.

Alexis paused. She looked at him square in his passionate brown eyes; she knew exactly how much he craved to be with her. She was confused. She was only one step away from being naked, but she couldn't seem to get her grandmothers' sermons of *legs open and babies popping out,* out of her head. The thoughts rushed through the very stem of her being.

Depictions of her sister fully developed with just three months left also cradled her mind.

With the scorn and confusion she knew she would receive from her mother was too much to consider, her lust had subsided, and her willingness to act on the knowledge of her true nakedness had then become a turn off. Whether it was God or grandma that was on her mind, she still had to face a horny Ricky, who wanted every part of her, including the kitchen sink.

Ricky sensed that something was wrong, so he quickly grabbed Alexis and pulled her panties down before she could even breathe. He quickly pulled back his shirt, which revealed his toned chest as his mind had raced to the finish line with the thought of his first shot with a virgin woman; it was an opportunity of a lifetime in the hood. It was like the golden belt of a championship boxer, having placed so many other chicks on his belt, in his mind, there was nothing better to brag about than the women whose heart he

was in a frenzy to take. Ricky Wilder was to be
notched on her mind forever, no matter how many
guys she may have dated afterwards.

Everyone remembers their first. He thought to
himself, because he couldn't separate reality from
fiction. He finished loosening his belt and Alexis
clearly saw the big bulge in his underwear. She was
taken back. She felt frozen in time. Her lust for him
returned and Ricky badly wanted to return the favor.
He picked one leg up after another as he took off his
boxer briefs. Fully naked and ready, he came in closer
to her. She pushed away again, but he brought
himself back over to her. He kissed her on the neck,
shoulders, chest, and thighs. He kissed her on every
muscle of her body as he slowly positioned his lower
body without warning to be symmetrically aligned
with hers.

Seething the conviction from her
grandmother's words, she panicked. She was unsure
of the new world that she was getting herself into, as
much as she felt that she wanted sex, she just wasn't
sure how to handle the aftermath of her decision.
So—she thought of some random quote that she
heard a televangelist repeat when she was flipping
television channels a week prior.

"Ricky, stop it. Stop it, Ricky, my flesh is weak,
but my spirit is willing." Alexis completely removed
herself from Ricky. She knew that she really wanted
him, but she was scared and afraid of what the future
was to bring, especially since there was no form of
protection in her line of sight.

Ricky was accustomed to women telling him
no and *stop it*. He went back over to her, but with a
little more aggression than the last round, he
playfully threw her to the bed, and was ready to reap
the rewards of his prey.

"But— but— Ricky you don't even have a
rubber. I can't get pregnant. Let me go." She pushed
him back.

Ricky backed up and opened a drawer full of
contraceptives, with an uneasy smirk, he asked,
"Which one would you like me to put on?" She was
relieved, but still felt bad in her spirit. It was a
dangerous feeling because, on the one hand, her flesh
was ready to give the goods to Ricky, but on the other
hand, in her spirit, she knew that the God of her
grandmother and mother would not be pleased with
her playing Russian roulette with her life.

She heard her grandmother's voice again,
ringing in her ear like clockwork. *"Once you lose it, you
can never get it back baby. Being a virgin is a precious
jewel to have. It gives you power and authority over the
wicked ones; surely, it is something to be cherished with
your husband."*

Of course, Ricky didn't hear her grandmother's
voice that rung in her head, the only voice he heard
was the smooth soulful sounds of R. Kelly's, *It Seems
Like You're Ready*, on repeat in his big bulky CD
player. Being the smooth player he was, he slowly
calmed her nerves.

"Hey, I know you're scared, baby, let me
handle this. I promise you. You'll be good. Everybody

has sex; this is how we really show each other that we care about the other. You know what I mean." He curved his wet pink tongue around his lips as he lip-synched a few of the lines from R. Kelly's song.

She was comfortable again and partially blanked out as Ricky took the initiative and administered a taste of foreplay. *I hope he doesn't hurt me. I hope this really feels like my home girls described.* With her feelings boiled up in ecstasy, she didn't know what was going to happen next. *Wait a minute, is he really about to take this to third base? Oh my God this Negro is bout to kill me.*

With the smell of Ricky all over her body, she began to scream. The pain and pleasure of the moment were building up something in her that she had never ever felt before, something that her sister had always warned her about. But after the first few minutes of pain, there was much pleasure to be had; she gave up the cookies, a sign of the beginning of her whole life crumbling down.

She didn't quite know whether to call it consensual or rape since she told him to stop once, then insinuated for him to use protection. Either way she thought of it, the deed was done after twenty-six minutes of painful lovemaking. The drumbeats stopped and reality for Alexis came back full speed ahead of her.

Ricky Wilder was satisfied, happy that he finally broke a virgin. He slipped out his phone and sent a text to his homeboys, he described every detail of his foray with Alexis.

Alexis, on the other hand, was more confused after the deed was done, than when she gave it up.

Only if I didn't let him take off my clothes, only if I was persistent with my no. Only if I didn't even come here. But I guess it was worth it. He loves me anyway. Yes, he loves me. She tried hard to convince herself of a reality that she only believed herself. She tucked herself in the corner of the bed, she looked away from Ricky, and she cried in silence. Alexis tried to figure out all that had happened. After all, she was the one that knocked on his door and sought him out for sex, but she just couldn't shake her grandmother's words, and she couldn't shake the thoughts of that one percent chance of getting pregnant or an STD advertised by the condom makers. She felt bad. Her flesh was weak.

Rude Awakening

It was the fall of Alexis's sophomore year and the last year for Ricky at Miami Carol City High. It was a mildly warm August morning. All the kids were back in school, and the seeds that were planted in early summer vacation were beginning to sprout one by one, as many of the teen girls were showing. A sad but true occasion, which seemed to get uglier every year, students with no care in the world during the hot summer months practiced risqué behavior and in the fall faced the penalty of their decisions, some chose abortion, while many others chose to keep it.

For Alexis, she didn't have much time to decide. Her sister was past due, yet in her eyes. Her sister was a seventeen year old senior pushing towards eighteen and would be pushing out a baby boy any time soon. Alexis, on the other hand, was fifteen and confused. All of her so-called hopes and dreams had vanished, and an already burdened mother of hers' couldn't figure out a way to feed two more mouths, with pampers, medical and everything anyone could imagine a baby needed to survive.

Brenda had already brought up the proposition for adoption if Alexis were to ever get pregnant.

"Girl, listen to me, and listen to me closely, Alexis, I can't handle another baby in this here house, so you better stop being mannish and keep your legs closed. I'm sure there is some well to do family out there that wouldn't mind taking in a baby out of wedlock. But my house is full; no more babies are welcomed here." Was the speech that Brenda had given Alexis.

"But how could this have happened? I thought we used protection every time." she whispered to herself as she slowly strutted down the hallway.

I can count on the number of times we did it. I believe it was twelve times, oh no— maybe sixteen times. I thought I remembered. I mean— after I lost my v-card, we were going at it every other night like rabbits, so for all I know, it could have been twenty more times that we did it, and I— guess that one of them times we may not have used protection.

Yep, that's right, Ricky was heading to a party this one night, and I was horny, so he said that we could like do a quickie. My dumb self was so in heat that I let him penetrate me without a rubber. I thought that he pulled out in time because it was quick in deed, but I guess some of the milky white slime ended up penetrating me as well. I am so stupid. Just when I thought I did everything right, I'm not ready for no kid.

It was like a month ago when the test strip came up positive, I cried and I cried in the bathroom. Toilet was still colored with yellow, and my heart just sank. Out of all the girls whom Ricky done been with, I had to be the one to get pregnant. I've heard of horror stories of girls getting pregnant on their first time, but we had done it multiple times. I trusted Ricky. He said he knew how to pull out.

But I was wrong, and I can only hope now that he doesn't pull out on his kid like the other men do in the hood.

Alexis eyed the man who helped make her pregnancy possible, and what she observed was terrible. Her man, with his tightened dreads and shiny gold teeth full of swagger, Ricky was kissing on another girl.

With pent-up rage, and built up steam, Alexis ran over to where he was, til' she remembered there was a tiny miracle that was forming inside her. She drew even closer to Ricky, he finally observed her coming, out of the corner of his right eye, and then like the promiscuous man he was, he pulled back from the random girl to meet Alexis halfway. He knew that if she got near the other girl, there would have been trouble.

"So, who's this hoochie you all kissing up on Ricky? Who is she? What? You done knocked her up, too." She was livid, although she knew that Ricky had his secrets, none that she was able to ignore, she never witnessed him cheating in action. Although many of her so-called friends were able to describe the furry lion with the big nose tattooed on his lower abdomen, she never wanted to believe that her Ricky got around that much.

"Naw, she cool, Lexi. That's one of my study partners. I was just trying to tell her something in her ear; it's so loud in this hallway. You know what I'm saying, gurl?" He pleaded for her understanding, but in the back of his mind, he wished he had been more careful.

"No, I don't understand, here I am carrying your baby, and you want to be out here with every girl who has an open door." She screamed.

"Listen here, you don't have to get all loud with me, I already told you to get rid of it. If you need the money, I'll pay for it. But Ricky Wilder don't got no kids; I don't even play like that. I ain't ready for no shorties anyway. I just like to mess around, and I know that the sex been good to ya, but babies just ain't where it's at for me right now, Lexi. I got dreams; I got bigger places to go. Kids just gone slow me down."

She paused for a second to catch her breath. Neither one of them heard the bell ring five minutes prior.

"What about my dreams, Ricky? What about my life, my future? I told you that I wanted to be a nurse one day, but having a kid is gone slow me down, too. But what are you saying to me, Ricky?" Her voice inched up a few levels again.

"Are you saying that we should get rid of this baby because your sorry tail couldn't pull out? I think that whatever the sex of the baby is, the kid at least, deserves a chance to dream, too. She stretched her feet towards her tiptoes to get a quick glance into Ricky's eyes; her heart could not believe what her mind suggested to be true.

"I believe that we should just chill, you know what I'm saying." He looked away from her; he tried to distance himself from the feelings he felt about her and the baby. In his heart, he knew he was wrong, but he always tried to keep what Michael Lewis said as the foundation for his pimping enterprise, "Don't have a baby with your prostitutes."

Although Alexis clearly wasn't one of Ricky's prostitutes, she was penned as what he would describe as one of the main products to build up capital with on his business plan. He looked at Alexis like the slave owners of old, he saw her not as a person, but as a commodity for trade.

"But Ricky," she drew a deep breath. "This is yours just as well, as it's mine. How could you just tell me to give up our baby?" Her feet silently patted the hallway floor, she waited for a response. And in her silence, she found a breath of strength. Maybe, just maybe Alexis had the tools to be an overcomer.

"First of all, you ain't even have it yet. Secondly, like I told you before, Ricky Wilder don't have no kids." He frowned, agitated that they were still discussing her pregnancy. "And all I'm saying is like; I ain't ready for that kind of responsibility. You know what I mean, like this just ain't the time right now, Lexi, I don't know how better to explain that. This time just ain't the time. That's it, end of story." He looked away from her; he felt a tightening in his chest. Another thing that he was told by Michael Lewis was to never let a woman see your weakness.

In the words of Michael Lewis, "If a woman sees an ounce of weakness in you, they will eat you up and serve you to the dogs for breakfast. Women don't need or want a weak man. You got to take initiative for what you want, but don't fall in the trap of weakness and despair. Even if you tapping that honey, keep that relationship on a professional level, every man got to let go them urges sooner or later. And the most important rule of pimping, don't get no skeezer pregnant, if you get her pregnant, then she pimping you.

A pregnant woman is lost inventory on my behalf, but not only is she lost inventory, my young stud; chick becomes a liability rather than an asset. Keep a raincoat on you, dog, believe me, you will save a lot of money."

As Ricky reminisced on what Michael had told him, he built back his confidence, his self-esteem, and he stood against the wall with assurance. He knew that his swagger alone would take care of anything that Alexis threw his way.

"When will it ever be the time? My baby is on a clock, and whatever it is, he or she doesn't have time to wait for you to pick up and be a man." She leaned into him.

Ricky could feel the hurt buried deeply between her eyes, but his pride couldn't afford for him to hold her, his pride couldn't even say the simplest thing, *I'm sorry.*

She backed away slowly. Tears had formed again, they moved down her face like a river. Maybe that's it, a river of life for both her and her unborn child. Maybe, just maybe, they were tears of forgiveness. However the circumstance, her eyes were swelled with the liquid fabric of her external being, or maybe, just maybe, they were tears of peace and baptism. A cleansing needed to take place for her life in order for her to be equipped to serve the life of another, maybe that was what Alexis needed.

"You know what, Ricky? I got to go. It's been real, but I just can't stand here another minute trying to convince you of the obvious. So here is my final message to you, there is a life with a heartbeat inside my body. I can't abort this child; my mother had me when circumstances weren't that great for her financially. She could have aborted me. She could have placed me on the chopping block, and she could have disowned me. But no, because of God's grace and mercy I stand here as a healthy, beautiful, and sophisticated young lady. And if you want to play those games, then fine, I'm keeping it."

The tension between the two couldn't have been more evident; that very moment would change their lives forever. No more was the power to choose life and death in the hands of Ricky, for that power had been reciprocated back to the one who would make that ultimate decision anyway, Alexis. But then again, was she really the one who played the Master's card, or was the power of life and death decided by the Author and Finisher of their faith? Is the power of life and death founded by the one who created the Earth in six and rested on the seventh? Yes, truly, the power of life and death is only prescribed by the Dr. of the Universe, and that's God. God is the captain of one's faith. Man has plans, but God has had eternity to decide on the outcome of all.

Alexis and Ricky parted ways, after a few seconds of eye-to-eye battle; they expressed every particle of non-verbal communication. Alexis somberly walked off to class, with her head held down, all she was able to think about was, *Mama was right, grandma was right. Men are the dogs. Men are deceptive and men are the last thing I want to be with.*

As she continued to straddle down the hallway, she recognized a couple of girls laughing at her. Their facial expressions said, "I told you so..." Alexis continued as she passed two more classrooms, she released her river again, with so much that was released; you'd think that the well had run dry. But she kept on as earlier before. Each tear pierced her dimples, her cuticles and pores had been mildly cleansed; beauty was now willing to participate in her moment of pain. Hurt had no meter to the tears it unleashed, hurt did not care how deep rooted the pain was. Hurt had one responsibility, to make one feel bad even in the most desperate and excruciating of circumstances. Hurt also can be a very rewarding experience for it also brings life, freedom, and the pursuit of better.

Hurt is also sustained by an underlined belief system that allows individuals to grow stronger. It helps to purge the weaknesses of mankind, at least, the ones who were not scorned by the hurt itself, but were relieved and released to do abundantly more than one would suspect.

In life there seems to be so many moments that you'll regret, I hated that day. That day back in 2004 when

Ricky Wilder showed me who he really was. I hated that day with a passion. I hated that day! I wished that day had never happened, but it did. I wished that day would have never developed, but it did.

That day was a turning point for my feelings about men. That warm August day that Ricky left me in the hallway; stranded, struggling, and afraid.

I don't understand the scenario of everything that was going down at fifteen, but I do understand that at fifteen I had a lot of decisions to make, and with those decisions, there was judgment to be had on both sides.

The Drums Play

It was another night of warm sex for Brenda, as two packs of cigarettes and two shots of hard liquor was not enough to relieve the stress and tension of being a new grandmother at thirty-seven, and another grandbaby on the way. The male she brought home wasn't just any man off the streets, it was the girls' father. At least, Alexis and Sabrina's father. Brandy's father was nowhere to be found, and according to Brenda's sexual history, she wouldn't know where to start. Alexis and Sabrina's dad escaped from Federal prison through some of his high up connects. But he knew it wouldn't be long til' the Feds would be back on his trail, so he decided to give one of his former employees a visit.

"Ma, who is this man, and why does he look like he got cancer or something?" Sabrina asked suspiciously. She knew that it was quite unnatural for her mother to bring suspicious men around the girls that early in the evening.

"I see she's grown up, and boy does she have a mouth on her. If she worked for me, she'd be pimp slapped, no questions asked. You still turning tricks Brenda?"

"I have mouths to feed, and you barely gave me a wet nickel when you were a free man." She reached in her purse for a lighter. Brenda rarely smoked in the house. In fact, she barely smoked at all.

"Yeah, you should be giving me royalties; I referred those men to you, not the other way around. You still belong to me Brenda. Maybe now you can finally turn me a profit for all the money I've been paying out to you."

Alexis entered the living room, she was curious about all the noise going on. Immediately, she recognized the man that was standing still in her living room with a hurried gaze painted on his deteriorating face. "Hey, I know you; you are that pimp who lived in the neighborhood and went to jail."

The man stood silent for a moment, and then like the switch of a light bulb, he said, "Well, this pimp is your daddy Alexis."

He stood there with an uncomfortable silence.

"What!" Sabrina gasped.

"I'm your father, too," he replied.

"Is this true mother?" Alexis retained her composure.

Brenda knew that it would boil down to her; she took an even greater puff. "I'm afraid so, honey. Michael Lewis is your and Sabrina's father. It's a long story that I dare not collaborate on.

"It's not a long story. It's rather simple. They are old enough to hear the truth; you've been doing tricks around them anyway. Truth is kids; your mother here is a whore. Your mother used to work for me before her and I had you two. She was something special, but just like you both; she had kids. After having Sabrina, she was no good to me, I can't make money off a pregnant woman, and I sure couldn't imagine sending my baby mama out there on the streets.

So I set her up in this little apartment here, rent free by the way, but I told her to make a promise to never reveal my identity to you two. I just couldn't stand you two knowing that we all lived in the same neighborhood, and didn't live together." He was silent again.

"I wasn't ready to be a father. I'm still not ready to be a father. It's just not in my DNA, and I don't know how to take care of no kids. I never had to change a soiled pamper in my life. I know you two are older now, but still—my life of crime does not allow me to be there for you two.

This is of course, not the first time I've been here; I just came at a different time. I watched you two girls grow before my very eyes at a distance, and your mother here would send me pictures from your birthday celebrations and special events."

"So, why are you here now, aren't you supposed to be in jail?" Alexis asked with an attitude.

"That's exactly my point. I'm here because my health has been failing and after the Feds lock me up this time, they may just throw away the key. I had to see you two and let you know how sorry I was before it was too late. I just thought that it was best that you two had a chance to see who your daddy was. Unfortunately for me, I never knew who that bastard was, and I'm sure you two probably feel the same way about me. No matter how you feel, I just want you two to know that I love you, I have always loved you, but this business is not for the weak. And having a family is not only a distraction, but also a weakness, and people out there that don't like me could try to hurt you to get to me. Some things I had to do for your own protection, but most importantly, it was just business."

"How could our lives just be business? We have feelings, too, you know? Why did we have to end up with the raw end of the deal?" Alexis pouted.

"He's not our father Alexis; this is just one big joke. Mother tell me when to laugh and for how long." Sabrina chimed in; she hurried to the backroom after she heard her baby boy crying.

Brenda could use a third shot at that moment. The stress became unmanageable. "I'm afraid that this is no joke. The man before you is your father, and I have to get some rest. Why don't you ask him all the questions? I'm done." She escaped to her bedroom, tears had swollen in her eyes, they dripped down to her toes. The pain in having her children hear him calling her a whore was worse than a ten ton piece of metal falling ten flights of stairs and flattening her body. She cried relentlessly.

Her mind went into overdrive, she thought about all the tricks she's turned over the years. Each sexual experience after the other like a drummer playing, louder and louder each memory took up space in her consciousness, the ooohs and ahhhs... all sounded alike, there was no distinct sound, just extra cash flow to keep the lights on and food on the table over the years. She had always been at the mercy of men, and her daughters have reaped the fruit of her sins.

Sabrina reentered the living room with her siren of a baby boy in her right arm.

She looked on at her deranged father with scorn, she learned of his past; and wanted nothing to do with him. She noticed that her mother had left the room, she was tempted to escort Michael out of their home, never to return. Just before she could speak, Michael must have read her mind.

"Listen, girls, I don't know what you two might have thought of me. I am no Saint. What you thought that I, your father, would have come in here like a knight in shining armor and make everything okay? Well, you two have it all wrong. That's just not me. I'm a criminal. I don't know anything else than how to get this bread through pimping. I'm sorry that you had to find out like this. But this is the truth. You two are so beautiful, and should be proud that you both have made it this far without me. As for your mom—" He hesitated to say, he stuttered for an answer, he scratched his head. And turned and looked passionately in Alexis's eyes, the keys to the soul.

"I still love your mom. She was my first baby mama, and she bore me two beautiful daughters who have now made me to be a proud granddaddy." He paused to breath. He succumbed to the sweat that pierced from his forehead down to his dimples. He picked a napkin from the table, and then, Alexis raised her voice to speak.

"Why come back now, what's in it for you?"
Alexis looked on at the man who she was to believe to
be her father, a light skin, frail looking man who had
all the years of life written across his face. She looked
on at him and hoped that she could have at least,
gotten one moment back that she missed him. But she
knew that particular wish was impossible. So, she
stood her ground, and tried her best not to let her
emotions get in the way of the interrogation she gave
her father.

Brenda snapped out of her pity party and
stood behind the hallway wall which led to the
kitchen. She'd been one courageous single mother,
but she certainly wasn't determined for her children
to find out about her sins like that. She ultimately
knew that her children had reason for suspicion, but
never in a million years could she have imagined that
the tales of her whoredom would be announced so
bluntly in her own home. It devastated her.

"Lord God if you are listening, I need your
help. I need your help Lord God. I've been depending
on men for a check, when I should have been
depending on you to help me keep a godly balance.
Lord God, please help me." Brenda whispered a
prayer; she hoped that her prayer was silent enough
to not be heard by her daughters and Michael, and
loud enough to be heard by God.

"There is nothing in it for me, Alexis; I just
wanted to see my offspring before the feds throw
away the key. You two are my seed, and I'm sorry
that we did not meet each other under better

circumstances." His cell phone alerted him of a text. It was one of his connects warning him that the Feds had his picture on the screens of millions of homes nationally. Clearly, it was Michael's signal to wrap it up as he somberly replied to the text, he realized that. That specific moment with Brenda and his daughters may be the last moment he will ever have with them.

"A text just came in that the FBI and US Marshall's are hot on my trail. I have to make a run or turn myself in, either way, I have to leave from here before a Calvary of thirty agents swarm on these premises. I've made these decisions on my own; no need in punishing you guys more. By the way, tell your mother that she'll always be my wonderful; she'll know what I'm talking about when you deliver the message." He rose from the table and briskly headed to the front door a little choked up and teary eyed. Michael pressed through. He left with him, millions of unanswered questions that were burning at the pits of his daughters' hearts.

Brenda held her tears as she heard the last words spoken by Michael. She was his *wonderful*.

*****

Brenda could recall the first time Michael Lewis called her his *wonderful*. They were on South Beach sipping on Martinis getting to know each other, and it was their first date. She was seventeen and Michael was twenty-one. She was quickly taken back by his seductive brown eyes, six-foot frame, broad shoulders, and high yellow toned complexion. That was back in the day when light-skin brothers were still 'in' and Kid from *Kid N Play* had all the ladies drooling after him. Michael also had that type of effect on Brenda; she eyed him like he was the Statue of Liberty, ready for him to ask her to take a tour of places on him that she did not see. She lusted after him, and as an eleventh grader and under age drinker at the time, she was sprung.

Everything Michael said to her that day was like Heaven on Earth to her. He couldn't do any wrong.

"Baby, I was wondering what you thought about getting in the water, it looks real good," Michael exclaimed.

"Boy you know that black folks can't swim." Brenda laughed a bit, she was tipsy from the third Martini.

"Speak for yourself, I for one can swim. You know they say that the ocean is God's gift to mankind to see his real beauty, power, and strength. They say that if you can really see the ocean for what it's worth, you've already seen the universe all wrapped up here on earth," he said as he chugged down a Margarita mixed with a cold beer.

"Wonderful," Brenda said without any logical expressions.

"Are you listening to me, girl," he laughed a bit. He knew that Brenda was either drunk or on the verge to being drunk.

"Yeah, I'm listening. You just sound all deep and all. I'm not sure how to handle you."

He looked into her eyes. "It's not your place to handle me. It's my job as a man to take care of you." He licked his lips and moved closer in her territory. He was good at tempting women. Brenda moved her head back closer to the beach towel. She wanted to kiss him, but was unsure of how that would have made her look on a first date, so she let her eyes do the kissing instead.

"I know you want to kiss me, don't feel bad because it's our first date, and let your body release what your mind has already prepared for me."

It was as if he could read her mind, and all she could say was, "Wonderful," which stirred a slight edge of frustration in his mind because even at the youthful age of twenty-one, Michael was still about his business.

She held back like the young girl she was. She thought that she was a flirt, but she was really scared inside. Maybe it was the drinks that had her nervous, or maybe it was Michael's smooth word choice. Either way, she knew that her mother wouldn't have approved of her being seventeen at the time with a twenty-one year old man. But she also knew that it was only a matter of fate, she liked Michael a whole lot, and after much teasing and conversations over the phone, she knew that she at least, owed him a kiss on their first date.

Brenda picked her head up from the sandy beach towel, shy and afraid she closed her eyes as she

took her right arm and reached around the back of
Michael's neck. He knew right then what she wanted
and did not hesitate to meet her half way.

"I could cradle your sweet lips for years to
come, girl. Where have you been in my life," he
jokingly announced with a laugh that followed.

Brenda pretended to also enjoy the joke, but
she was too consumed by the liquor til' she didn't
quiet comprehend their moment on South Beach in
perfect ninety-degree Florida weather.

"Wonderful," she barked out again, and then
fell back on her beach towel with eyes shut.

Needless to say, Michael was a little tipsy
himself, and barely caught on to Brenda's partial
awareness, so he called her *wonderful* because every
time he made out a complete sentence, she would say
wonderful. They later laughed and joked about the
whole ordeal of them both being drunk and not
making sense of anything at the time, but he never
stopped calling her his wonderful. Even when
Michael was cheating and brought her into the fold of
his pimp enterprise, Brenda still believed that she was
the most wonderful woman who Michael had ever
met. Needless to say, that bond for which they had
formed on South Beach was the glue that kept her
sane when it came down to working in the business
of prostitution for Michael Lewis.

With all fairness at seventeen and leading into
her early twenties, Brenda was a hot commodity. She
often had guys running to open doors for her and
wanting to introduce her to their mamas. But she was

in love with Michael. She couldn't help that her Milky Way skin, smooth round bottom and buttercup lips drove the guys wild. Needless to say, her beauty would be her down fall, as she pursued prostitution as a substitution for college, not that she had the money to go to college, but she had the grades to potentially acquire a few scholarships. Brenda was hard headed, raised by foster parents; she wanted the fast life, fast money, fast men, and a chance at being a star.

Brenda got into the world of prostitution because Michael gave her a good sales pitch that she couldn't resist. He told her that doing a few tricks was only temporary and one of the fastest ways to an early retirement. Michael was a smart man. He had charts and graphs lined up that showed her how she could turn enough tricks to put a half a million in the bank by the time she was thirty.

Besides the sales pitch, Michael always played on the fact that he was her first love, and she said that she would do anything for him no matter what. And so she did, when she first started prostituting, it was a scary proposition for her. Her mind ravished with what if questions. *What if I get raped? What if I catch a disease? What if a guy doesn't pay me my full share? What if Michael turns his back on me? What if Michael doesn't love me anymore? What if my mother finds out? What if I get caught by the police?*

It wasn't until after a few men had visited her at a hotel that was setup near the beach, that the process became a lot smoother, and many of the what if questions left her mind altogether.

She always made sure that the guys used protection and she always was tested on a monthly basis. Brenda was one of Michael's best girls after a while, and she was turning more tricks and more money faster than any of them could count. But no matter how many men she opened up her legs to; she couldn't seem to open up her heart to no other man besides Michael Lewis. She never had any real dreams in life, and whatever dreams she may have had, they practically faded when she became pregnant with Sabrina.

"I will always be his wonderful," Brenda whispered to herself. She chalked past the memories, gazed on to her daughters and her grandbaby. *Oh, God, how blessed I am to have healthy children. They will always be my wonderful.*

Don't Play With Dogs

"Push, Alexis, push," were the screams of the male doctor in the ER who held her right hand as Alexis's grip became much tighter, Brenda held her left hand, while her own hand was at the verge of losing circulation at the astonishing strength that pulsated from Alexis's core being.

The female doctor was at front and center of Alexis, she played the role of comforter. It was like a case of good cop, bad cop. The male doctor of course, was the bad cop, he screamed for her to push and get it over with. The female doctor told her to take her time, she filled her head with lullabies of, "It's going to be alright, and it won't be this painful the next time around." It was the perfect blend of pain, pressure, and comforting words that she needed, if she wanted to have a successful baby.

Sabrina, Brandy and Brenda were all there to cheer her on, but the father of her child, Ricky Wilder, was no-where to be found. Of course, he found a way to weasel out on the baby's birth that he disapproved of. His excuse was centered on a random family member that was supposedly sick for which he said he had to go out of town to see. Of course, his excuse didn't hold up much weight with Alexis, but she didn't bother to fight him either.

"Lord, please help Brandy to wait to have sex til' she's long gone and out of my house. Help her,

Lord. so that she doesn't follow into her sisters and my footsteps." Brenda whispered a prayer over the moans, groans, and panicked laden atmosphere. Certain that God couldn't hear her over the orchestra of noise, she wanted to cry out to the Lord herself like when Samuel cried out to the Lord on behalf of Israel to save them from the hands of the Philistines.

"But I can't push anymore. I'm tired and this baby hurts," Alexis complained.

"You have to keep pushing, Alexis. It's for your own good and the good of the baby," the male doctor said with conviction, his hands painted red. He was ready to get on with the next step, he was ready to launch the baby to Earth, its new temporary home.

"Keep pushing, Alexis, you can do it. You were made for this. This is the natural order of life." The female doctor shared a smile. She eased the tension and pandemonium, Alexis thought about everything that she went through in one year, and she decided to lay it all on the table. And with one big push, silence ensued. The male doctor released his hands from Alexis. Brenda released her grip as well while Sabrina stepped forward. The female doctor hurried around to her vaginal opening and with one more push from Alexis, her baby had successfully arrived. The baby cried, screamed, and took the first gulp of breath. Everyone except the doctors seemed to be suspended in a slow animated type of matrix.

The male doctor cut the umbilical cord and the family waited for confirmation of the sex, "It's a girl." The doctor's cheered, as the female doctor clutched the baby in the palm of her hands, washed her up a bit and handed her to Alexis. Alexis was happy to hold a new life in her hands. Her baby was named Kita. Kita was a healthy coffee-colored baby; she weighed in at six pounds, two ounces, and nineteen inches long. She was just a beauty to be seen. She was truly God's gift to Alexis Carter.

She looks just like her father. Her nose is wide like his, and her eyebrows are almost as thick as his too. Alexis thought to herself. Sadness grew in her heart as the absence of the baby's father was reminiscent of the lack of her own father in her life. *Where is that bastard anyway, why couldn't he have at least, shown his face?*

"Lexi, is everything alright?" Her mother sensed the mood shift, and with her motherly instincts, she knew why, but dared not to ask at the time.

"I'm okay, Ma," she lied. She wanted Ricky to be there, and she wanted revenge. She missed him; ever since she announced to him that she was pregnant, he didn't want anything to do with her. She felt like yesterday's trash when she knew that God created her to be a treasure. It's not like she was sleeping around with every other guy, she often told herself, she tried to justify where she went wrong with Ricky and her relationship with God.

She sort of knew in her heart where she went wrong, she only wanted him for sex. At least, that's what she believed when they first started dating. But feelings and passions gnawed on her inner self, and what she first wanted from Ricky was not enough, she wanted every part of his being. The two did become one, and her intuitions for a strong fulfilling relationship had kicked into overdrive.

*****

"Have you heard from the boy yet?"

"No, Ma, I told you he said he wasn't coming around. He said he's been busy working on some project."

"Girl, I will go and speak to his mother. I know she raised that boy better than that." Brenda lost her temper. "I don't know what's wrong with these young Negro boy's these days. They fill your cups with foolishness and afraid to take care of their own. My Michael took care of me. We may have been struggling, but he kept the rent paid up and made sure to give me a few dollars to keep a meal on the table. Your boy is a natural born dog! If I ever seen one, he probably think that he's God's gift to women and can handle not taking care of his seed, I ought to slap the joker when I see him."

"Ma! Ma, its okay I'm thinking about putting Kita up for adoption anyway. I believe that Kita deserves better than this." She pouted, she was afraid of what the future would tell for her and her baby. It's was two weeks since they left the delivery room and the bond between her and her child had been stronger ever since Kita began to suckle on her mother's breast.

With every drop of milk that tipped into her daughter's mouth, it was a drop of joy and pain, for the joy was the connection, the pain represented the possibility of losing her. Alexis couldn't stomach the thought of losing her first child, but it may have been a necessary evil in order to give her child a life, which she couldn't provide.

"There is no grandbaby of mine being adopted, the Lord will make a way and we will keep this child just like Sabrina's boy is growing to be healthy and strong. You will just have to get a job and put the no good ex-boyfriend of yours on child support. We will apply for food stamps and have this to work in our favor. It was a fifty-fifty decision to lay down, Lexi, so part of it is your fault to blame. But God don't make any mistakes, just miracles, and this baby of ours is a miracle. She ain't did nothing wrong to nobody, no need in making this little child suffer. She's so cute, got a head full of hair and eyes twinkling like the midnight stars. Don't you give up my grandbaby, Lexi. You hear me? This child stays with us."

Alexis heard everything her mother had spoken, but at the tender age of sixteen and a child herself, she couldn't quite grasp the meaning of responsibility and what it would entail for her to work at a minimum wage job while in school at the same time. Her dreams had not only been crushed, but they had been shattered. Her hope to one day be a nurse had all but faded away. *I guess you can be anything you want to be, as long as you don't have a baby.*

Sabrina walked in on all the commotion as she held her little Andre in her hands; she tried to rock him to sleep in the room, but all the noise seemed to keep him up and crying.

"What's going in here, my baby's tired, but you two apparently want to keep him up."

"Child, go back to your room, I'm the head mother here, and this is my house." Brenda said playfully. "I'm just trying to talk some sense into your sister here; she's talking about giving her baby up for adoption."

Alexis chimed in. "But, Ma, weren't you the one that originally suggested that I give her up through adoption. I could clearly remember you saying that you have too many mouths to feed and can't afford for another child to live here." She stared at her mother and waited calmly for a response.

"Girl, I know what I said, but I said it out of anger and frustration. I said it when I was struggling to pay the light bill and the food stamps didn't come in yet, so I had to spend a little extra on food. So you are right, Alexis, guilty as charged." Her voice raised a note, anger spewed, she was unable to comprehend why Alexis brought back up a sour subject; at least, to Brenda, it was long gone and done with.

"Lexi, ain't none of my grandbaby's going to no strange folks homes, at least, not if I have some say so in the matter. Those kids get to those homes and they are seen as dollar figures to the parents who adopt them, all the while being abused, molested, and raped right under the nose of HRS. Some of them kids walk around looking spooked and their own parents have the nerves to label their kids as dumb and retarded, at least, the parents that keep their kids just so they can get an extra check from the state. Ya'll see them hoochie mamas round here dressed better than their kids. You think they getting child support from their men?"

She continued her rant with a strong conviction, "No, they getting State money, they don't work; they don't care about them kids. They just keep popping them out like mutual funds. Happy to add another social security number to the house to get more money, I have never been that way. Never thought about claiming ya'll as retarded. Well, Brandy I kind of questioned." They all snickered as she leaned forward and playfully popped Brandy on the left shoulder.

"I never filed for child support, and I never, ever thought about giving you kids away. You all are my blood. I can never think of doing such a heinous thing. But it's only been by the grace of God because if the State would have come here and thought that I was unfit as a parent, they would have taken each one of you, no questions asked."

"Okay, Ma, we get it. I'm sure once Lexi thinks about it; she'll make the right decision."

Brenda interrupted, "There is only one decision, we keeping this child." She put her foot down as she glanced at little Kita. And with her small skeletal frame, Kita seemed to have smiled right back at her, of course, the baby had no knowledge of what was going on around her, but she looked just as happy as she could be.

Alexis didn't say another word, she squirmed in her chair as she listened to her sister Sabrina and her mother argue about the future of her and Kita. *I don't know what to do, Lord, this needs prayer.*

*****

"Why haven't you been answering my phone calls Ricky, your daughter is getting bigger and she could use a fatherly figure every once in a while. Whatever beef you got between you and me, that's between you and me. But Kita is your daughter. She needs you." Alexis said softly on Ricky's porch, she could smell the stench of sex whiff to her nose through his screen door. *That's probably why he's not letting me in. He got some hoochie in there, probably getting her pregnant.*

"Listen Lexi, I got business to take care of, ain't nobody told you to come around here unannounced. Secondly, I don't even know if that child is mine for you to be talking about me spending time with her. And third, even if the child is mine, I told you to get an abortion anyway. I told you I don't have any time for kids."

She was furious, but kept calm to keep from exploding, "You know that I was a virgin when I was with you and I haven't been with anybody since. And since you speak of her not being your child, you can come with me to the clinic and take a DNA test. It won't be a long process. It's short, sweet and to the point." She waited. She also heard the movement in the backroom. She knew it wasn't his siblings. They were still in school.

"I don't have to take no dang on DNA mess; I know who I done busted in. You think you the only woman trying to get me to take that test? I got three other chicks just like you crying and screaming that I'm their baby's daddy."

"So, are you?" She asked without hesitation.

"Chick please, I know my stuff is good, but I also know when to pull out." He grinned.

"You sure about that, cuz you sure did a number on me and knocked me up." She didn't care to join in on his sudden sense of humor. She couldn't believe the man or boy she saw before her slightly hidden behind the screen door. She could make out most of his frame, three gold teeth in his mouth, pants nearly dragging the floor, wife beater undershirt on and the smile that she first fell in love with. Then she took another glance at him and noticed the slit in his boxers. Part of his *drill bit* was peeking out and memories of her and him came back alive in her memory bank. She still loved him, and the lust for what she felt in bed when she was with him was overwhelming.

"You got anything else to say chick," he snapped her out of her dream like state.

"Yeah, I'll see you tomorrow and I'm bringing the baby over." She stood her ground and remembered why she went to his front porch in the first place.

"Yeah, whatever trick, I got other things to handle. Come round here if you want to, you may not like what you get."

"Yeah, whatever Ricky, you ain't nothing but a liar, cheater and manipulator. You're a dog Ricky, a real wild dog that will pay for your sins." She let loose a few tears; Ricky didn't notice or care to notice through the screen. He lashed back at her.

"Why you got to get all religious on me now. You weren't talking about sin. Well— never mind. Anyway, if I'm such a dog, why you messed with me? Didn't your mama tell you not to play with dogs cause you might catch fleas." That was the dagger for her. She wasn't able to take anymore scolding that day.

"Thanks for reminding me, I'll be taking my S. T. D. test tomorrow." She turned around and left his porch in anger, she rapidly paced towards her home.

She heard him, in the distance, he professed that he was clean, while he inferred that she was a female dog, under the term that individuals often call each other out of anger and spite. She continued to pace faster toward her home; anger, frustration and guilt tore her up inside like a bad case of acid reflux.

Ten minutes after leaving Ricky's house, she arrived on her own front porch. "Mama, I'm through with men." Alexis announced, she cried and shook unnaturally; she gripped the door to walk inside.

"Well, what do you mean honey, what happened? Did somebody hurt you? Did you let some man put a hand on you?" Brenda could not believe her ears. She hated to see her children upset; she almost wanted to cry with Alexis.

Sabrina and Brandy raced out of their rooms; Kita and Andre were in the back competing for the best crier competition.

Alexis picked her head up and said firmly, "Mama I'm through with men." And just like that, the three became silent. Even the baby's cries became more of a whisper, as Brenda took a quick glance into Alexis's eyes to see the seriousness and disturbing nature of her comment.

Without another word, they each just stared at each other. They knew that something in their lives was about to change, but how it would affect each one of them, they were unsure, but something, something potentially ungodly and unnatural was brewing in the air. They each took one more look at each other, and then a deep breath as if they were all being held on a string that was being directed by the same puppet master.

"Well, what can we do to help Lexi? I know that you are hurt by this Wilder boy, but that's no good excuse or reasoning to give up on men. We are all women here. We are here to help you Lexi, only if you let us." Brenda remarked with sincere concern.

"I don't need anybody's help right now; I just want to be left alone in my room."

Brenda didn't want to push the issue any further, Brenda let it go and said, "Okay baby, but dinner will be ready in an hour. Sabrina, check on the babies for me. Brandy, stay here in the kitchen with your mother, you and I need to have the talk. You know the one about the birds and the bees."

Alexis was long gone from their presence by the time Brandy and Brenda began talking in the kitchen, while she was alone in the room, she was playing back her disgust for men and curiosity for women, all the while she reminisced on the image, she saw of Ricky that previous hour. Once again, she thought about the moments they shared and the slit in his pants that exposed his reproductive organ. She lusted after that once more, and then she contemplated on the type of feeling she would have had if it were the reverse.

Alexis naively wondered how she would feel if she was staring down the sultry legs of a woman, she pictured a woman's reproductive organ. She saw her sister's naked, she never thought twice about it. But with fresh battle scars from her altercation with Ricky, her mind conjured up images of her own nakedness and the potential gratification she would feel with being with another woman raced through her mind, it crept down to the very crevices of her soul. Then she was startled by the lullaby of, "Dinner's ready sis." by non-other than Brandy.

"Okay I'll be there in a minute." Alexis spoke with an attitude, not because dinner was ready, but because she was going into the deeper parts of her fantasies, and her curiosity to explore the deeper parts of a woman came into question. As she battled in her mind between the visual of the slit in Ricky's pants exposing the part of him that she loved and the visual of one of her best friend's Sylvia naked at the slumber party she was at month's prior.

   She remembered every curve; every crease on Sylvia's body, Alexis was quickly aroused by the dimples in Sylvia's breast and flat iron chest. Alexis remembered, she remembered it all. Interrupted again, by her mother that time, she decided to give her fantasies a rest, as she washed up for dinner.

Curiosity

"**W**ake up, wake up girls, it's time for school. No need in prolonging the inevitable. Come on Lexi and Brandy, time for school. Sabrina's fixing some grits and bacon for you two, Andre and Kita are fast asleep. I'll wake those two up a few minutes before you all leave. Hey, Lexi. You mind if I speak to you for a second?" It was more of a demand rather than a question. She heard the seriousness in her mother's tone. Alexis complied without rebellion.

"Brandy, you can go ahead and wash up while your sister and I talk for a minute."

"Okay." Brandy replied with a smile. She always did what Brenda told her to do without hesitation.

Brenda looked around the corner to make sure no one was listening; then, she looked Alexis up and down til' their eyes met at the center. "Is everything okay with you, girl? I know that you had a stressful couple of months dealing with that fool of an ex-boyfriend, but you can't come around here talking about being through with men and stuff. So tell me baby, what can I do to help you?"

Nothing, I've already made up my mind. "I don't know, Ma. I'm good, I guess. I was just having a bad day. Ricky and I kind of got into it, and he hurt me real bad. He called me the b word as I was leaving and didn't have anything nice to say to me." She let her head down as she felt her stomach growl; she hoped that the conversation was going to be over in a moment's time, she tapped her feet on the floor with a slightly subtle frustration.

"Listen here, honey, some men can be dogs, and it's in their nature, especially here in the projects. But then, there are some men who are like gentle giants, they will sweep you off your feet; woo you with flowers and save you as a gift for marriage. I've experienced every kind of man imaginable; believe me when I tell you that. The majority of the men I've been involved with were dogs, but I knew it. I played into their games because I also have needs. Both financial and others I dare not discuss, you have a child; you know what I'm talking about.

So listen, all I'm trying to tell you is don't give up on men. Men can be wonderful creatures if you let them and as long as you play the game right, you will always get what you want. They think that they always get what they want, but listen to me, sweetie, and listen well. Girl, you have power crafted between the center of your legs. Don't let any man abuse that power either, use that power to your advantage. Now I'm not saying to go out there and be a whore like me." She paused, disgusted by what slipped off her tongue. She was embarrassed and thought about what Michael had said, she slowly walked away. Then turned around and said, "Lexi, find you a good man. God made men for a purpose, so you celebrate and find you a good one. Don't make my same mistakes. Trust in the Lord, He'll get you the right one."

Mama maybe well-intentioned, but at Miami Carol City High, she is certainly misinformed. There are no good men there, just thugs and want to be players. Maybe the great White Knight will come and save me from my misery. Besides, I don't have time to think about boys. I got school and a baby to take care of, and I'm only in the eleventh grade.

*****

"Carter, Alexis Carter why aren't you writing down the notes that I have placed here on the board. This may be the first day of school for this semester, but you do have a pop quiz on tomorrow." Her teacher shook her head in disbelief, and then grunted something to herself. *These sorry Negro kids will never learn to take responsibility for themselves. She's probably one of those girls on the long list of students with kids. God, help this generation.*

Alexis was in a daze; she thought about her best friend, Sylvia, she was bound to see her in the following class. She reminisced on the memories she had of Sylvia four months prior. Her fantasies expanded once she went to bed, and she felt much pleasure in rewinding the events that sparked her friend, Sylvia, to get naked at the slumber party.

It was a girl's night out, and Alexis and her friends made it a game night at Sylvia's house. Sylvia's parents were gone for the weekend, so she had the house all to herself. At first, Sylvia thought to have an all-out party, and invite a couple of guys from school and the neighborhood, her plans were to have booze, loud music, and a good time. But because Alexis and their friend, Monique, were both pregnant at the time and couldn't drink, Sylvia decided to just have a game night between the six friends.

The girls played the popular board games such as Monopoly, Candlyland, Uno, and Checkers. Then, they watched some of the classic eighties throw back films like 'Trading Places' and 'Coming to America'. The girls were exhausted by the time midnight had hit, but one of the girls had suggested that they play Truth or Dare. Of course, the other girls protested at first they said, "It wouldn't be any fun without guys being around because normally weird things can begin to unfold as truth or dare begins to heat up."

"I think that it's better that we don't play with guys, they tend to get too aggressive. You feel me?" one of the girls voiced her opinion.

"But isn't that kind of nasty to play with all girls, you know what I mean, I can't see myself kissing no girl like that," Alexis admitted.

"Shut up, Lexi, let's just have some fun and see where this game will take us," Sylvia said.

"Hey I don't know about ya'll, but I'm out." Monique insisted.

"Why," the other girls except Alexis said in unison. "We haven't even started yet."

"I know, but this just seems kind of weird without guys playing along." Monique shook her head, she was deeply uncomfortable with the idealism of playing with all girls in the game of truth or dare.

"That's what got you pregnant now; you took a dare and went all the way." The girls burst with laughter. Monique did not find it to be funny, but she knew that there was some partial truth to what her friend, Claritha, had mentioned.

"Okay, gals, are ya'll in or ya'll out?"

"I'm in," each girl said, except for Monique and Alexis.

"Always the pregnant woman ruining the fun, it's just an innocent game, won't anybody get hurt, and the two of you won't get pregnant again," Claritha said with pleasure as the other girls roared with laughter once more. That time Monique loosened up a little bit and joined in with the chorus of giggly girls.

"Hey, so are you two in or are you out?" Sylvia asked, she twisted her hips to and fro and waited for a response. The other girls looked on with partially dropped jaws and ears pointed to the ceiling in anticipation for Alexis and Monique's response.

"I'm in." They both said with heavy eyes which were yielded into peer pressure.

"Bout time, and since you two took so long to make up your minds, how about you two go first.

"Okay, that's cool with me," Alexis said as the consummate spokesperson for herself and Monique.

She looked on to Monique to start the game and asked her the first question.

"Truth or dare, Monique?" Monique stared down at her waist as if she had a crystal ball between her legs that would of told her which one to pick.

"I'll pick—" The girls eagerly awaited her response. Monique hesitated. Finally, she looked on to the other girls whose faces were grim with anticipation and decided to make a decision.

"Come on, girl, it's not rocket science," Claritha said.

"I'll pick truth." Finally, she chose a path to take; she released a sudden breath. She felt at peace with her decision.

"Okay, girl, is it true that you slept with both Rob and Junior before you got pregnant?" Alexis licked her lips; she desired to ask her that question for weeks.

"Wow, you had to go there huh, Lexi. Yes, it's true though." She turned around in disappointment.

"Ouch." The other girls chanted. "So who is the baby daddy?" Claritha asked.

"Wait a minute, it ain't your turn to ask a question," Sylvia silenced Claritha.

"Lexi, truth or dare," Monique gazed on at Alexis. She hoped that she'd pick truth so she could dig up some dirt to ask her.

"Give me truth," she replied with a smile.

Bingo. "Is it true that your mom's be having men's over all times of the night?"

"Boo...," the girls shouted.

"Wait a minute that's not fair, Monique, this is supposed to be about me, not my mama." Alexis knew that there was no real way out of that question because if she didn't answer they would believe that it was true, and if she did answer, she had to tell the truth. She felt that there was no way around her mother's sins, and it wasn't getting any easier for her as most of the people in the projects knew about Brenda making a living on her back. But it still didn't make Alexis feel any better about the situation.

"Yeah, it's true, since you had to take it that low about my mama Monique."

"Oh, so your mom's a hoe." Claritha suggested without biting her tongue, the other girls laughed at their newly appointed ringleader. Alexis was ashamed in the process.

Sylvia tried to dispel the comment; she noticed the disappointment that was evident in her best friend's eyes. "Okay whose next, let's move on with this game. We don't have all night."

One by one, each girl obeyed and delivered their version of silence.

"Sylvia, truth or dare my sista'?" Claritha gazed at her friend with a devilish demeanor. Sylvia caught a whiff of Claritha's motives and decided to choose dare.

"Sylvia, I dare you to bark like a dog while pinching Lexi at the same time." Claritha held back what she really wanted to dare her to do, she figured that she would play that card later.

Alexis chimed in, "Wait a minute, that's not fair. How could you get her to hurt me in the process of her own dare?" she pouted like a girl scout not able to sell any cookies.

Claritha had heard enough. "Stop whining, Lexi, dang girl this is just a game. So take your little pinch from your best friend and keep this game in rotation. Where are the men when you need them?"

"Woof...Woof..." Sylvia barked like a dog and delivered a light pinch, she fulfilled the demands of her dare. The girls were ecstatic, rolling all over the couch as they dropped the freshly microwaved buttery kernels of popcorn. They couldn't recall ever seeing Sylvia do such a thing; she was normally the uppity one of the group.

"So Claritha, what's it going to be?" She felt offended by Claritha's odd request. Sylvia wanted payback, and she wanted payback quick.

"Girl, I choose the truth, nobody in here has any dirt on me."

Sylvia looked around at the girls, then back to Claritha as she tried to find something to ask of her, but the truth was she didn't have anything, at least, nothing that stuck. *Oh, what a dummy I am, I have nothing on her.*

"Is it true, Claritha, that you used to piss the bed up until the age of five?" she asked, figured that she might as well wing it since she didn't have anything solid.

"Girl, you just trying to make up stuff, and of course, that's not true, like I said, you don't have any legitimate dirt on me."

One of the other girls stood up to claim her share in the game. "Stephanie, truth or dare?"

"Give me a dare," Stephanie said, "This game is boring. I need something exciting to do."

"Okay, well, I dare you to kiss Claritha on the cheeks." The girl requested.

"What, I ain't about that homo stuff now. I said a dare, but I didn't mean that."

"Haven't you kissed your mother on the cheeks before?" She asked with a rough smile.

"Yeah, but that's my mama. It's a kiss out of love, not some game that forces me to kiss a random girl. I mean Claritha's not random, but you know what I mean Tia."

"It's just a girl, and it's on the cheeks, what is she going to do, lighten up a bit," Tia said.

Claritha did not protest a kiss on the cheek from Stephanie, as the game continued the request became even more awkward. The girls were daring each other to do things that they would not have normally dared to do or ask of the other. Tia opened up the door to something more than a simple game of truth or dare. She opened up a spiritual unseen world of homosexuality; a legion of demonic spirits had their eyes on each one of the girls who were participating in the game, what was once just friendly fodder, had turned its head to a deadly spiritual disease, *lesbianism*.

"Sylvia, I dare you to do a strip tease and move around this pole right here between your entertainment center like a stripper." The girls looked on with pierced eyes and high shoulders, they were curious to see if she would really do it.

Without argument, Sylvia unloosed each article of clothing, she took her time in the process, and she was filled with doubt, embarrassment, and pleasure all at the same time. Who knew she could get that much attention from her friends. Lastly, she was down to her bra and panties. The girls looked on with eager anticipation, neither one could contain themselves as that particular dare had been the greatest dare of the night as they each were constantly pushing the envelope to see what the other would do.

Sylvia forced both hands to her back as she unstrapped her bra, she revealed a solid thirty-two C; she then lingered along and forced her hands to reveal the lower part of her equation. The girls looked in awe as if they had never encountered the thing in which was between their very legs as well. Then, at a moment's chance, Sylvia danced around the pole located between the entertainment center and the kitchen area. The girls could not will themselves not to look; their curiosity got the best of them as each one captured mental images of Sylvia's nakedness to store for later retrieval.

For Alexis, her later retrieval just so happened to be the day her and Ricky Wilder argued on his porch and her daydreaming of Sylvia's pure black bottom while in class. Her imagination stretched for miles, as she never before had such intense thoughts and feelings for a member of the same sex. She daydreamed on Sylvia's perfect curves, her perfect C cup, and cocoa butter skin with a Halle Berry smile. Alexis literally drowned in her imaginations.

*****

"Alexis, surely you aren't paying attention to me in this class. I don't know what's got your mind so warped, but here is a bathroom pass to get it right. You have five minutes young lady, five minutes. The bell will be ringing in fifteen minutes; I need you back here before the bell rings so I can give you your assignment. Is that clear young lady?"

"Yes, Ma'am'." Alexis moped and rummaged to the front of the class as if she was still pregnant, she dragged her feet and blew kisses at Sylvia in her mind. She was happy for the restroom pass. She wanted to text Sylvia while in the bathroom, but decided against it, she didn't want to seem either desperate or crazy for feeling a certain way about her friend, and she sure wasn't ready to tell Sylvia that she was sexually attracted to her. Her feelings for Ricky Wilder were still intact, but her curiosity for the same sex had intensified.

Spoilers

"Girl, you beaming like a pot of gold, what's up, Ricky done brought you back into the fold, or somebody done knocked some sense into that no good Negro?"

"I'm just high on life. I feel like this is my new beginning."

"Oh, yeah, what you smoking on?" Sylvia batted her eyes, rolled her neck and took a deep portrait of her friend. She never witnessed her friend smoke anything a day in her life. *Why would she start smoking now? That can't be true.* Sylvia thought to herself.

"I'm just good, you know I don't be smoking like that, especially with this baby around. I have been feigning for a blunt though." She smiled, she thought about all the stress that instantly seemed to be removed the moment she put her hands on a blunt and lit it up. She even loved to watch the smoke that left her mouth and polluted the air in the process. Ever since she was under the influence of Ricky Wilder, she took a liking to smoking a blunt, a few *Black&Milds* here and there but never cigarettes.

"Well, what got you so—I don't know, you just look happier. You don't look like you've been looking the past couple of months. Tell me what it is that got you all excited and looking extremely happy in the process." Sylvia reached for her keys; it was as if she had to call the Coast Guard to find them through the sea of junk she had lugged in her purse. Finally, the silver edge from the tip met the light and she grabbed her key so quick you would have thought it was an inhaler for her asthma. When they entered her home, she and Alexis settled in on the couch. She reached for the remote that controlled the television; Sylvia powered the huge fifty-eight inch set.

Sylvia came from a family of well-educated and middle class means; Sylvia was the only girl out of Alexis's friends who did not live in the projects. She lived a couple of blocks away from Alexis on Northwest Thirty-fourth court, which were also a few blocks shy of Carol City High.

"So what do you want to do next, Lexi? I have some board games we can play, we can surf the Internet, and of course, it's always moving so slow. My parents just have dial-up. We don't have DSL yet." She released her pent up disapproval with a heavy breath.

"Just be happy to have what you got, we don't even have Internet in our home, not even a computer, we have to go to the library for everything, and hope we can dial up somebody to take us there because I hate taking the bus. All those old men be on the bus drooling and staring at my booty. Those old men stare me down like I'm a hot sausage dipped in juice." she laughed a bit at her own comment.

"You funny. That's why I like you. You keep it real." Sylvia kept flipping through channels, with so many choices she was unsure of what to choose for their entertainment.

Alexis continued where she left off. "Girl, I'm for real. Those men do be looking all disgusting. I'm talking about forty and fifty year olds, Sylvia. Then, this one dude, oh Lord, he was so disgusting and obnoxious. This one dude, had to be in his fifties, came from the front of the bus to the back of the bus trying to holla at my girl, Kesha, and me. I mean dude looked like straight bum material, gurl. How about he was talking bout some, 'let me get a piece of that chocolate pie, before daddy comes home for supper.' I was like what?"

"Ha-Ha-Ha—" Sylvia giggled hysterically, her head swayed back and forth, she cried with laughter.

"I'm serious, girl, and then he had the nerves to fondle himself in front of both of us, as if he was wearing a pair of Michael Jackson's gloves, how disgusting." Alexis looked on at Sylvia in horror. The giggles stopped and the room became silent.

"Uh, Lexi, are you ok, girl, did that man try to touch you two?" Sylvia asked. She continued to study her best friends face. She wanted to put down the remote and give Alexis a hug, but she decided to wait for a response instead.

"Naw, girl. That man ain't try to touch us, and if he did he would have met my blade that I carry inside my purse at all times. My mother taught us girls to always have a blade handy, she said that if a man tried to touch you without your permission, and if he pulled his pants down, she said to make no hesitation to cut it off and let him sing to the choir."

They both united in hysterical laughter. Neither of them could look at the other and keep a straight face. They just laughed and laughed, they moved the couch a few inches back in the process.

"So--- what you want to do? I thought you were about to pop in a DVD for us to watch."

"Don't be silly. I'm still crunk off all that laughing we were doing a few seconds ago. You always got your lil' stories to tell, and they always be funny. So, how's the baby? I know she got to be like eight months old by now."

"Yeah, she'll be eight months in about a week. That girl is getting big, seems like my baby grows like an inch a day. She definitely takes after her father. That boy got some strong genes. And something even stronger meshed between his two thighs. That boy made me dance like a professional. He had just the right formula to please me."

She looked down for a moment; her heart was saddened at the thought of the betrayal and agony that Ricky Wilder put her through. She could count on one hand the amount of time that he actually spent with his daughter.

"Yeah, I miss Ricky. I wish I didn't, but he was kind of like my first love. You know what I mean?" She picked her head up, and tried her best to look cool. But deep down, she wanted to tear up.

Sylvia sat in silence, not a word could be freed from her lips, and she shook her head at the thought of another young black man walking out on his child.

"Most dead beat dads don't mind the pleasure; it's just that they don't want to prescribe to the responsibility that the nurturing and raising of a child brought. So—the easy thing for them to do is to run and run hard from their baby mamas." Sylvia was dually disturbed, she hated what her friend had to go through.

Many men idolize their kids as some sort of trophy notched on their belt of superficial accomplishments, while their kids grow up in a repetitive cycle of poverty, drugs, and violence without a father to stretch forth his hand in their time of need and trouble. There in deed are a few good black men in the hood not bound by the stereotypes, but unfortunately for Alexis and Kita, Ricky Wilder was up to no good and he had no training as to what a real father does for their offspring.

"Remember I told you about that no good whore of a boyfriend Zack. That boy just about runs me to a special home where the people eat lettuce for breakfast and take shots for dinner. And believe me; I'm not talking about the kind of shots that are served at the bar. "

"Of course, I remember that scoundrel; you instant messaged me like every other hour about his dirty ways. Wasn't he in our Biology class last semester?"

"Yeah, well, to make a long story short, Zack was my first love and he broke my heart sharper than a charred piece of glass. My reflection of him was never the same."

"Girl, I'm through with men." Alexis bowed her head.

"Lexi, what you talking about, as much as we hate those cheating dogs, at the end of the day, they are surely a woman's best friend." Sylvia remained calm and optimistic; finally, she kept the television on one channel for longer than fifteen seconds.

"I know, Sylvia, but like you've never had thoughts…" She held her breath, afraid to say what she had on her mind, afraid for what her best friend may have thought of her.

"Thoughts about what?" Sylvia pressured.

"You know thoughts about…." Alexis was still too embarrassed to say how she felt, those feelings that she wanted to convey had plagued her for a couple of weeks. Every time she closed her eyes, she seemed to visualize herself with the same sex, yet she knew deep within herself that the thoughts were wrong and not of God, but the pleasure she felt playing on her flesh made her question if the word of God was right or just a bold-faced lie.

She seemed to have given herself a pass on the context of sex before marriage, which was written in the Scriptures, but sex with another female was an area of uncertainty for her considering how it spoke on such carnal acts as being an abomination.

Alexis could not stand herself for that moment because the one person that she was normally able to trust and rely on with awkward situations such as the one she faced, was also the one woman who could judge and ridicule her for the rest of her life. So, like most would have done while faced with such trauma she decided to stay in her shell, she decided that it was the best choice for the both.

Sylvia was persistent about what was bothering Alexis, so she kept trying to push an answer out of her.

"Sylvia, I'm not going to tell you, so leave me alone already! Okay." she fumed at the mouth.

Sylvia backed off and decided to change the subject; she noticed that her friend had enough of her badgering and prying.

"Well, there doesn't seem to be anything good on television, I have some special videos in my room that we can watch." Sylvia said with a sly grin.

"What do you mean by *special* videos?" Alexis questioned, slightly thrown off guard by the emphasis on special.

Like a shy schoolgirl, Sylvia back tracked to explain herself. "Well, my parents you know got these tapes. Basically, they have a whole collection of porn." She decided to be blunt about it with a straight face.

"I guess my parents watch the videos for fun because they are fun to watch for me. Of course, they don't know I be borrowing their videos." Sylvia turned away; she didn't want to see Alexis's reaction to her newfound love for *special* tapes.

"Uh-- that's nasty. You be watching your parent's videos. That's just absolutely disgusting Sylvia."

Sylvia's features puffed up in shame; that was surely not the reaction that she was looking for. She knew that Alexis made a mistake in her take on the tapes. She decided to explain herself. "No, silly, these tapes are not with my parents on them. They are of other people. Lexi, are you crazy, I would die before I watch my parents doing it on the tape or in real life. I thought I just clearly said that they were porn videos."

"Oh, my bad, I mean—you know your parents could be starring in their own videos." she let out a loud giggle, ashamed that she would have even thought the tapes bared the nakedness of Sylvia's parents.

"So, we are going to be watching tapes of other people's parents on video?" Alexis asked out of sarcasm, she had previous experience in the area of pornography, she just tried her best to pull her best friends leg.

"I don't know, I don't—." she grimly looked at Alexis. "I don't think about that stuff, it's all just entertainment. I'm sure that most of the porn stars aren't married and I'm really not watching them and thinking about how many kids they got."

"I know, I just was trying to get a reaction out of you, needless to say, it worked." she laughed at her best friend. Sylvia didn't seem to find the humor in it.

"So, do you want to watch the videos or not? Have you even seen these types of tapes before?"

"Yeah, I don't mind watching the tapes; my hormones feel a little heavy anyway. And, yes, I have watched pornography before. My big sister and I watched it like two years ago or something like that. There was this wretched white woman who was dressed up like a housewife, she and a black dude were in the act. That particular video was boring to me, so I haven't seen any porn since. Maybe you have some better videos for us to indulge in."

"Maybe, but I know that the housewife was a part of my parent's collection, I know not to show that one today."

They each headed to Sylvia's room where she proudly took fifteen DVDS out of a shoebox, which was hidden under her bed. Each DVD had its own theme, plot, and characters just like the big screen movies. They both unanimously picked the doctor and the nurse video and watched each intricate detail of the flick.

"I knew that you'd like this video."

Alexis did not have a response. Her eyes were still glued to the sin that was on display. The video led both of their minds into worlds they could not have imagined before, and it brought them into a realm of new and stronger demonic spirits.

The scene with two women sharing intimacy with each other played richly on the screen, both Alexis and Sylvia rolled their eyes back in lust. They imagined a woman of their choice that they could share the greatest of their deep dark fantasies with. And before they knew it, they both shared an intimate kiss.

"I'm sorry-- something got a hold of me. I did not mean to do that." Sylvia backed away frantically; she reached for the remote and paused the video.

Alexis followed suit and gave her apology, but deep within her heart, she knew she wasn't sorry for kissing Sylvia. She was sorry that they had stopped so suddenly. She wanted more, and she liked what she felt.

"Well, girl, I got to go," Alexis announced, she was embarrassed by the moistness of her undergarments and even more embarrassed that her sudden affections for Sylvia could not be hidden behind her nonchalant smile.

Sylvia knew that something was up, the passionate kiss that she shared with her best friend was different from any other kiss she had with a guy. She knew that. That particular moment was neither the time nor place to tell Alexis, so she picked up her keys and prepared to take Alexis home.

"Are you ready, Lexi?"

"Yeah," she said nonchalantly, even more embarrassed by her ordeal, she hoped that the wetness would not show through her clothes. To her surprise, she was still dry on the outside, but for

Alexis, nothing seemed to come easy as she walked out the door, she took slow, rhythmically induced baby steps. As they closed the door to Sylvia's house, they each looked back; both realized that they had opened the door to something else. Something so evil, so unnatural. That its very nature is a lie from the *pits of hell*.

*****

What exactly is lesbianism? Is it some sort of spirit that resides over the earth and is loosed on those who turn to pornography? I mean. That sounds kind of silly, but yet it seems like that's the type of connection that happened today.

Grandma always said, "The devil loves to entertain, and even God's people, the very elect are fooled by his tricks, magic and sorcery. His legions of demons are on one assignment. That assignment is to kill, steal, and destroy God's people by any means necessary. The greatest lie that he has used to corrupt the moral judgment of individuals has been through the lure of homosexuality."

I never figured what grandma said could be so true. Most times when I visited her, I just figured that she was just making conversation like any other older person; but this way I feel about Sylvia, my best friend, my boon coon, my ride or die chick, this way I feel about her could not be explained any other way. The girl has certainly piqued my interest, and only God himself will be able to know if I can be saved from these feelings I got for her.

Sylvia's Request

It was a Sunny day on Miami Beach. School was out early, and all the kids from Miami Carol City High were edgy. Some were wrestling with their boyfriends, while others chose the beach to pick up unsuspecting girls, grill out, and have a good time.

Alexis, on the other hand, was home alone with both her one-year old baby and her sister's baby. Her daughter was growing fast, but still was not fully weaned off the warm suction of milk that streamed from Alexis' breasts during periods of nursing her. Alexis did not imagine that. That would be the life for her, a young beautiful teen with babies to watch at home while everyone was at the beach.

"Hey, what you doing?" Sylvia smacked her teeth on the other line without a care in the world; she was putting the final coat to her toenails while watching a syndicated episode of *The Fresh Prince of Bel-Air*.

Alexis responded. She tried to juggle a decent conversation and baby duties at the same time. "I'm here changing my sister's baby and putting my daughter back to sleep. This is no fun, Sylvia. You mean to tell me that this is what I have to look forward to for the rest of my life while that no good boy of a man sleep around with a bunch of heifers with no real sense of responsibility!" Her anger did not help in aiding her daughter to sleep; it actually did the opposite. Her baby girl cried and her sister's son cried right after.

Screaming and wailing was what the two children were known for, it was too loud for Alexis to continue a respectable conversation. "I'm gone have to call you back. You hear these baby's in the background. Bye."

"Hey, wait, can you come over later?" Sylvia asked with a half-smile that could have been seen through the phone.

Partially annoyed and tired of juggling tears from both babies, Alexis briskly said, "Yeah, I guess." She said without thinking of her mother or sister's plans for later that day. *Shoot, if I'm taking care of these babies now. Surely, somebody can keep an eye on these children later.*

"Okay, see you soon." Sylvia hung up the phone with pleasure, she was happy to know that she didn't have to be home alone in the evening. Her parents were set to arrive two days later. Her parents set sail on a cruise to the beautiful beaches of Nassau, Bahamas for their anniversary.

Babies, babies, babies, I wonder what Ricky is doing anyway. That no good Negro is a clown. The boy ain't gave me a dime for milk, pampers or formula. He just don't know how to take care of his seed. He talk a good game, but his wallet must be on empty. Sabrina's baby daddy ain't that much better, but at least he foots the bill here and there. At least he comes around every now and then.

Cookies

"Glad to see that you have finally made it, I started to get a little worried about you. I was thinking about that man who you were talking about being on the bus with the other day. I was hoping you didn't run into him. I was hoping you didn't have to pull out your blade or something." Sylvia smiled as she escorted Alexis into her home, Alexis had arrived just shy of five hours after their initial phone conversation, and as the clock rolled to six in the evening, the growls and churns of Sylvia's stomach could not take another minute without some sort of sustenance.

"Girl, you will not believe the drama that my mom and sister Sabrina put me through. They just don't seem to care about my social life. So, when they got back to the house, they each told me stories of other places they needed to be, I quickly had to remind them that I was home all day, watching the kids. They have to understand the fact that I'm a single mother not a housewife." Alexis paused for a break, relieved to take a sip of the cool bottled water that Sylvia had placed in front of her.

"So, how were you able to escape? I know that your mother can be a control freak, but it seems that Sabrina should be more understanding, especially since it's her son."

"I know, right. That's exactly my point. Sabrina normally takes after mom, whatever mom says,

Sabrina goes with the flow. I hate that, they are like twins in a sense. But mom, of course, is the mastermind." Alexis swirled around in her seat; her knee barely missed the edge of the bar.

"Well, sounds like you just need to chill, girl. I'm sure motherhood has to be like a fulltime job in itself."

"Tell me about it," Alexis said definitively as she crouched down in the chair, she looked for a gesture of sympathy from her friend.

Sylvia didn't notice Alexis's change in posture, so she quickly changed the subject. "So what do you want to do tonight?"

"Well—uh--I have a couple of hours to chill til' it's time for me to get back home." She gazed intimately into Sylvia's direction; she hoped that Sylvia noticed her signal, she was sending.

"Well, we can always start out by watching a little television. But first, girl, I have to get something to eat." Her stomach bent all the rules, as it continued to growl for attention.

"Yeah, food sounds good to me. What you got to eat?" Alexis ate a few hours before, but most of the turkey and cheese sandwich had worn off.

"Well, I got some TV dinners, you know I can't cook, yet. I even burn up popcorn if I ain't careful." Sylvia turned towards the freezer; she opened it up and discovered a grocery freezer selection of frozen foods. She didn't realize how much her parents had stocked up for her while on their trip. That was partially because she was eating out every night, while eating yogurt and cereal for breakfast and lunch respectively in that order.

"Cooking is one of the simplest and relaxing tasks that you can undertake. It's all about the rhythm, and you just have to have the right rhythm when you cook. Forget reading directions, my grandmother would throw in all kinds of stuff and the food was to die for."

Sylvia didn't say a word.

"Sylvia, it's kind of like when you first get broken in, at first it's hard to get into a rhythm, but after a while you begin to like it and can't get enough of the motion from love making. That's just how cooking is, it may seem a little hard at first, but it becomes easier and easier, especially if you got some Crisco around. My mother uses Crisco like a crack head hits a crack rock."

"I'm not a virgin no more so I know all about the motion, ever since what's his name and I dated. He took that away from me. I thought I told you about that."

"I don't remember. You be talking about a lot of stuff. But anyway, since you not a virgin and all, then, you obviously know what I mean about getting that rhythm."

"Yeah. That rhythm done got you pregnant and many more years to deal with a trifling dude that don't give two shades over Miami about you." She caught herself. "I'm sorry; I shouldn't have taken it that far."

Alexis tried to brush it off, but the rage she felt swelled up inside could not be hidden behind her fake smile.

"It's cool, girl. That's life. Negroes have been impregnating us black woman and leaving us to fend on our own since the time of slavery. Not that many of them wanted to back then, but when you had slave masters wanting to put the best breeds together like we were animals. That's just the way it happened. Of course, I'm not making any excuses for Ricky's behavior, but I'm just saying, we are all a product of our history, no matter what them folks try to teach in them history books." Alexis paused to breathe; she was always a lover of history.

Alexis continued. "Gurl, if you ask me, them projects I'm living in look like some old plantation housing development. But enough of that stuff. Let me give you a quick cooking lesson since you done got your history lesson for the week."

Sylvia smiled, grateful that Alexis didn't take her comments as hard as she perceived she would.

"Hey, you got some eggs and cheese in the fridge?" Alexis questioned, while Sylvia opened her refrigerator to find an abundance of eggs and cheese ready to be eaten.

"Yeah, here you go." She handed her the full twenty-four pack of eggs and the package of cheese.

"Ok, girl, get me a cast iron pan and some vegetable oil."

Sylvia did as directed, she put a fire to the pan and she lightly greased it with vegetable oil; they waited for approximately three minutes to move forward with the rest of the recipe.

"Hey, you see the pan getting hot?" Alexis asked, as she scrambled up the eggs with cheese in a separate bowl, ready to be poured in the pan.

"Now take this bowl I have here and pour it in that pan." Sylvia tensed up at Alexis's request. "Oh, and bring down the heat a notch."

Alexis noticed her friend's nervousness engraved all through her face, so she went behind Sylvia and helped her scramble up the eggs. With just a small touch from her body to Sylvia's there was an immediate awakening.

The kitchen wasn't hot enough for how Sylvia felt about Alexis, as her nipples protruded through the white fabric of her t-shirt; she hoped her best for them to disappear into her t-shirt as if they never came out for a peek.

"You see that, it's all about rhythm." Alexis noticed Sylvia's sudden arousal, and she too was aroused by the familial flowers and perfumes that were comforting Sylvia's neckline. As they slowly and rhythmically stirred, Sylvia turned back to look at Alexis, she was desperate, all she wanted was a kiss, the same kiss that she'd experience when they were playing truth or dare. The truth spoke passionately in both of their eyes, they wanted each other, and they both knew it.

Their fantasy was interrupted by the eggs that were crying for their attention. "Ooh, what's that smell?" They were burning up the eggs, Sylvia had turned her back, and Alexis wasn't paying the slightest attention to the eggs. If anything, all she could think about were the eggs inside her, begging to be fertilized. Begging to produce once more, begging for nine more months. But she knew that part could not be possible with a woman, Sylvia had no seeds to plant, but a kiss in Alexis' mind, a kiss can go a long way.

"Gurl, you done burned up the eggs." Alexis shook her head.

"Did not," she replied like an innocent child.

"Did too," Alexis came back at her in the same manner. And then, without another moment's chatter, they each broke into hysterical laughter.

"You are surely not a good instructor in the area of cooking."

"And you are no chef either, now we have to throw these eggs away."

"I will take out one of those TV ready dinners, what kind would you like meatloaf with mashed potatoes, meatballs, and spaghetti, chicken with broccoli, or pepperoni pizza with brownies?"

"I'll take the meatloaf."

"Good because I'm in the mood for some meatballs and spaghetti, both dinners should take about forty-five minutes to cook." She looked on at Alexis as if the chemistry the two just had did not even happen.

Alexis couldn't help but feel tormented about the whole moment, she relished the desire she felt for her friend while the guilt she felt about being with a woman had also triggered a depressed reaction. Because she didn't want to push the issue, she decided to go along with whatever plans Sylvia had for the rest of the night.

"Ok, so the food is in the oven, lets' watch some television." Sylvia flipped through the channels as they finally decided on a program to watch. Of course, they chose 106 & Park on B.E.T. The girls were having fun dancing to the latest music videos and laughing at some of the comments of the host.

"That's my joint, Omarion is so cute."

"Yeah, he is so adorable. I want to marry him." Sylvia looked on at the tube, she knew that her dream of a future with Omarion was one that was saddled by the millions of girls who had watched him perform live on stage and on television.

Sylvia stood up for the next song that aired live, the number three song on 106 & Park. It was the blazing sounds of 'Jesus Walks' from one of her favorite new artist, Kanye West. "This dude is going to blow up, I'm telling you, Lexi, he really brings something different to the rap game, and who would have thought you could make a song about Jesus in the rap game and still keep your street credibility."

"Yeah, he alright, we'll see. I done seen many rappers come and go. That's probably why I stick to R&B; at least they usually get a second album. And did I tell you how fine Usher is to me. Oh, do I have a confession to tell."

"Lexi, you tripping. The food is almost ready. I can smell it. Let me go check on the timer right quick."

Sylvia rushed out of her seat, checked the clock on the oven. It read exactly ten minutes, and then she rushed out of the kitchen and nearly bumped her knee on the stove. She did not want to miss the rest of her favorite music video.

The video was over and the food was ready to be taken out of the oven. Sylvia paced herself. She put on a glove and carefully removed the dinners from the oven. She slit the plastic as instructed in order to let each meal cool down and continued to cook a few more minutes as instructed.

"Alexis," Sylvia yelled out, "Time to come and eat."

"Bout time." Her stomach had growled a bit, but neither had really noticed since the television was at its loudest. "I'll go ahead and pray. Dear Lord, God we thank you for this food that we are about to receive for the grace and nourishment of our bodies, in Jesus name I pray. Amen."

"Amen." Sylvia said in agreement, and in one big swoop, she had a mouth full of spaghetti, some even dripped down the side of her lips like the Niagara Falls. She had been waiting all evening long for that moment.

"So what's for dessert?"

"I don't know, I can check out what's in the pantry or something. What do you like?"

"Well, I love brownies and ice cream. Of course, my grandmother can throw down on some sweet-potato pie, but with times like these, there is nothing like some warm, partially moist, richly filled chocolate chip cookies. Gurl, if you know how to make them, they will have you feeling like you can touch the moon."

"I don't think I have any chocolate chip cookies," Sylvia remarked as she eyed down her plate that was already seventy-five percent finished.

"Do you have some flour?"

"Yeah," she responded with a confused look on her face.

"Okay, so do you have some milk, salt, butter and some brown sugar?"

"Yeah--" she wanted to say something else, but was quickly cut off by Alexis.

"Okay, well what about vanilla extract and of course, chocolate chips."

"Well, I don't know about all of that, but I can check the refrigerator in a second."

"Okay, cool, if you have some chocolate chips, vanilla, and of course I know you have eggs for days. I can teach you how to make some cookies."

"Are you sure about that?" She questioned Alexis with a subtle concern; she hoped that she wouldn't burn anything else up. Upon finishing her meal, she looked into her refrigerator as instructed and to her surprise, there was a whole new pack of semi-sweet chocolate chips sitting in one of the drawers at the bottom of the freezer, and she found the vanilla extract on the side pouch. She closed the refrigerator door and then surfed the pantry for all the other ingredients, and sure enough, they were all there.

Alexis finished her meal, and then stood up to assist Sylvia. She instructed Sylvia to get the roller for the dough and the two had at it with mixing the ingredients. They played in the dough without a care in the world, they licked the raw dough off the others' finger.

"I can get used to making cookies. It's so fun." Sylvia said, more relaxed than she was the previous ten minutes.

"Well, the oven should be done with pre-heating; I believe that these cookies are ready to be baked." She took a flat pan and spread a cookie sheet across it. She also placed sixteen cookies on top. She couldn't wait for the ten or so minutes it took for them to be ready."

Sylvia still had a little of the raw dough on her fingers. She motioned for Alexis to move forward and consume the raw dough from her middle finger.

"Oooh that feels so good." Alexis moaned. Sylvia felt the same way, but decided not to release the pleasure that was built up inside her. But as Alexis continued to consume every bit of the raw dough left on her fingertips, Sylvia couldn't take it anymore. She placed both hands behind Alexis's head and swooped in for the kiss. A kiss she had been longing for all night, a kiss that was a part of her unspoken request.

The kitchen was getting hotter with both their excitement and the smell of the cookies. Alexis was smart enough to let go and quickly turned off the oven. Alexis put one of the gloves on, then she quickly took the cookies out and slammed them on the stove, she did not want to miss the moment. She grabbed Sylvia's hand and began to kiss her passionately on the neck. Her knees had buckled and for the first time in a long time, Alexis felt like a woman.

Her eyes were opened even greater to her true passions and she was happy to know that she could share those passions with her best friend in the world.

They headed to the bedroom, and forgot all about the cookies. They took their time as they explored each other in a more intimate, more perverse, more ungodly way.

"Lexi, do you want my cookies?" Sylvia said with a deeper, raspier, more seductive tone that had ever been heard from her by Alexis.

The two girls lay side by side, naked and heavily in heat, "Well, I thought you'd never ask."

The two baked up something that was not suitable for the oven, they shared in each other's passions in a design that was ornately outside the will of God. The fervent lies from the enemy were all they could believe, as Alexis was marking her transformation to a life of lesbianism.

This is not a Charity

"**W**here were you all night, young lady? You didn't even come home last night. I called your cell phone at least a million times. Would you like to tell me what's going on, were you at that boy's house again making another baby?"

Only if she knew, I was making something else under the sheets. "No, Ma, I was at Sylvia's house. We were watching this movie and we kind of like fell asleep on it. I'm sorry, Ma."

"Well, your baby girl has a sorry woman for a mother, leaving us here at the house panicking because you did not make it home last night. Girl, go take a shower, you smell like puberty all over, and your hair is in need of a wash, too. Get on out of my kitchen, then come back when you are fresh and cleaned up."

What's wrong with this, girl, has she lost her mind? Lord, please help her not to get pregnant again. Lord you know I can't afford one more mouth to feed. Some tubes will be tied around here. Men these days are too eager to spill their seeds wherever they can. Trying to get a man to pull out on time is like trying to get your order right every time in the drive thru line at the Burger Joint, it just ain't happening.

*****

"That's the spirit, now you look like the beautiful daughters I've raised. I'm taking you girls to church. Lawd knows we some heathens and we need to be saved."

"But, mama, we never go to church, why the sudden rush now?" Alexis looked on at her mother, as if her mother had totally lost it. *Maybe she's bipolar.*

"Listen here and listen to me good, Lexi, I need somebody to help me to keep everybody legs closed, and that includes myself! And there ain't no better place than the four walls of the church. My mother kept me in the church, and then I strayed away and popped out you and your sisters. Don't get me wrong, you girls are a blessing, but I just don't need no more grandbabies crawling around this here house, in these little old projects. There just isn't enough space or money to make accommodations for anymore children."

Sabrina slid her head around the corner; she was awakened by all the chatter and commotion that took place in the kitchen.

"Mama, what you fussing about this early, it's only seven in the morning and you already about to wake up the babies." Sabrina reprimanded her mother, but she knew it wouldn't be too long before Brenda would come back at her with a sweet taste of fury.

"Listen, sweetie, before I have to slap the snot out of you, I have decided to take you girls to church. You girls are going to learn about the Lord just like my mama made me. Now I know that I haven't been the best example of holiness and righteousness, but I would not be a good mother to you and your sisters if I didn't take you all to the house of worship." She paused and then stretched her hands up towards the heavens.

"You think I enjoy being on them stamps, waiting for when the government decides to give me some new stamps in order to feed ya'll chilren. Do you think I like this kind of life, stuck here in these sleazy projects, home of where all the skeezers live?" She rolled her eyes as she took a quick breath, Brenda was on a roll and Sabrina wished she hadn't butted in on her and Alexis.

"Listen, girls, this right here is a dead end type of life, believe me, you don't want this. I dream of the day I can walk into a house that I can call my home. I dream of the day I see a mortgage payment. I'll be calling the bank before it's due. I dream of a well-managed yard with beautiful palm trees and sunflowers. I dream of the day I could see you two walk across that stage of not only high school, but also college. I have never been to college. But that future can be for you two. Now you both have to be an example for your younger sister."

"But why church, Ma, there's more heathens in church than in the projects." Sabrina said without any real hardcore facts, she based her whole theory on general perceptions of the church, specifically the black church.

Alexis chimed in. She figured that it was one of the few opportunities that Sabrina and Brenda would be in disagreement, "Yeah, that's right, Ma. Morgan down the street goes to church all the time with her mother, yet she got twins on the way." She poked her lips forward. She assumed that she had won the battle; she took a short breath with a wide smile.

"Listen here, sweeties, her getting pregnant did not have anything to do with church, and the heffa got pregnant because she wasn't paying attention to the very Scriptures that the word teaches."

Mama is a heathen, too, how dare she judge somebody and is guilty of the same thing. Sabrina shook her head in disbelief.

"What word ma?" Alexis asked out of curiosity.

Brenda could not believe her ears. "Oh, my gosh you don't even know what I'm talking about. I'm talking about the word of God, Alexis; His word can be found in the Bible." She exhaled for a second, and then took to some nervously heavy thoughts.

"Sabrina, find me a phone book. We are going to find a church that is open tonight; we are going to church young ladies. And that's final."

Not another word pierced either Alexis or Sabrina's tongue, for when they heard their mother say that it was final, they knew to keep quiet or duck for cover because something would have been thrown at them if they insisted on speaking.

Finally, Brandy entered the kitchen. She caught the tail end of the conversation, her mother was sweating profusely, so she asked, "What's wrong, mama, why you all wet in sweat, and why is Sabrina and Alexis over there all hunched over looking like some Chinese dolls?" She scratched her eyes while she eradicated any cold in her eyes that was left from a wonderfully deep sleep she enjoyed. Brandy's dream was filled with boys, Angels and Mermaids.

Brenda was restored to her normal self. "Now I know that you don't know much about what was going on in this here conversation with your two older sisters, but I will shoot it to you straight and tell you what it's going to be one time without any back lip from you or anyone else in this house. I will be taking you girls to church; tonight we are going to somebody's church. As soon as you girls get home from school, for which all of you are late right now. But as soon as you girls get home from school. I need you to all to shower up, put on your best clothes and we're heading to somebody's Bible study this Thursday evening." She paused for a moment, and she looked at the greatest three gifts that God could have ever sent her; Sabrina, Alexis and Brandy.

When Brenda looked in each one of their young and flawless faces, she was looking at an image of herself when she was in her youth. Just with that moment she captured her beautiful daughters, she knew that her anger towards them couldn't last long. She loved them with all of her heart, and knew that it would only be a matter of time before each one of them was out of the house and on with their separate lives, it was the casualty of time. Time always had a funny way of bringing back memories of the past, while brutally pressing forward in age towards the future.

"I will check the phone book to find the exact time. In the meantime, you gals better hurry up and get out of this house for school. I'm sorry, sugas, but I ain't made anything for you all this morning." She gritted her teeth, embarrassed by her mistake. Although each of her daughters qualified for free meals at school, Brenda always insisted on at least sending them off to school with a good breakfast. She was that big of a believer in the types of selections that her children were given for breakfast at the school. Lunch was even worse, but she felt that she could at least live with knowing that they had two good meals every day.

"If you all get ready fast enough, maybe you can still catch some breakfast from the school. Otherwise, my hands are tied, you know them stamps don't come back on til' the first of the month and that's in a few days. Right now, we are stretching girls. I have just enough formula and cornmeal for the babies. Their bellies will be good and full."

"I think I still may have a few dollars on my card." Alexis chimed in, her first few words in minutes.

"Oh know you don't. I had to let Mr. Henderson borrow your card for a few dollars in cash, and your card should be maxed out like the rest of us," Brenda said, in fact, while she feigned for a cigarette. She was disappointed with the fact that she could not light one in the house. Of course, she didn't want the babies to develop asthma or worse catch pneumonia. Even with the love she had for her grandbabies, she still would rather the comfort of being able to light one up in her own home, rather than outside like all of her other nosey neighbors.

Alexis, in the meantime, was saddened to hear that Brenda had sold off the rest of the money she had left on her food stamp card; she purposely saved that money for such circumstances. She knew her mother's habits of smoking a pack of cigarettes a day, gambling, and a few alcoholic beverages here or there and her coveted losses at Bingo nights would run her food stamp card dryer than a stale pretzel.

Brenda had never been able to keep money on her food stamp card for longer than a week, even though she received approximately three-hundred dollars a month. Of course, the girls knew that she didn't just use the food stamps as a bargaining tool for food, but it was another way for her to get cash loaded to play the lottery numbers with the hopes of becoming an instant millionaire. Of course, Brenda never analyzed the odds of hitting the huge Florida Lottery pots; she had more of a chance of being struck by lightning ten times in Florida than to win the lottery. But she played and played anyway. She gambled away her children's resources for food and monies that could have been used to help them get out of the projects. Unfortunately for Alexis and her sisters, Brenda was always able to justify her habits by saying, "It's stressful with a house full of kids and no father here to help. I should be able to have a few vices."

Brenda had never really been a fine example for her children, although she was no junky in the sense of being a crack head or on meth, yet her addictions did lie in gambling and cigarettes. And dissolving precious resources away from her family was no better than a crack head stealing to get another hit. This was particularly one of the reasons why her request for them to attend church had been both odd and strange. Maybe Brenda's daughters would receive their answer soon enough, even if God had to tell them himself.

*****

"Girls, are you all ready for the church house?" Brenda yelled to the top of her lungs.

"Mama, I don't want to go to church."

"Who said that?" Brenda immediately took offense. "Is that my little Brandy complaining about not wanting to go to church? Child, I will whoop you til' the moon turns blue. Girl, you better soak up them tears and get your rotten behind ready for some good preaching. You ladies have exactly ten minutes. And by the way, I couldn't find anyone to care for the babies, so the babies are coming, too. Make sure their butts are cleaned, make sure the milk is warm and right and, of course, keep an eye on your sister before I twist her arm."

Brenda left the hallway and sat on the kitchen table. She shook her head with displeasure. Her tears met the fake wooden table lamented in a cockroach-covered skin. That particular style of table was a staple for the projects. For Brenda, she rarely received any houseguest, well, at least not the type that sat with her at the table. Even then, most of her male houseguests cared nothing for the decorum of her apartment, but they cared everything about the decorum of her fully figured body. That barely looked a day over thirty. Of course, Brenda had that shared gene that allowed many black and brown people to look and age well, despite their actual age.

Of course, some still tend to look older than others do at the same age based on drug abuse, stress, and life circumstances, but for Brenda, most would not have been able to articulate that she birthed three children and already took on grandmotherly duties.

Her cries were silent. The girls could not hear her. It was a moment shared between her and God.

Oh, God, help me to find my way. Lord help me to be a better parent, take me away from my whorish ways, Lord help me to just be satisfied with one man. Lord, I pray for my grandbabies and Brandy. Let them be the ones that break this family cycle.

Oh, Lord. I am a failure, I had all these kids out of wedlock and now my kids are having kids that they too can't afford to take care of. Deliver me, Lord God, from my wretched addictions. Take away the gambling, Lord. Take away the cigs, Lord. I need your help, God, more now than ever. I can't live in these projects forever. Help me to find a better way, oh God, rule and write me in your book of life, oh God. I want to change. I believe that I can change. But change seems to come so hard at times that I feel like I'm spinning my wheels. Please help to mold me and secure me in your word, oh Lord. My mother raised me to know you father God and I have been going astray a long time.

Lord, I pray that them folks at that church don't be quick to judge my ways, but that they be quick to help. Lord God, I just need you now more than ever, I need you like the summer rain. I need you like when I was in labor and in pain. Help me, Jesus. Help me to control these feelings. Help me to bind these urges like my mother used to teach me when I was growing up.

Save my babies, Lord God, save my babies, show them where true love comes from because I'm certainly not the right candidate. Save them precious, Jesus, save them before you save me if you have to. I can no longer live my life this way. I want to give it all to you, but I just don't know how to. I'm a sinner. I'm a big sinner. How could you ever take me in? I done did a lot of crap, slept with plenty of men. Lied to my daughters, sold my body for a few short dollars. I want to change Lord God, please help me before it's too late. I give up; I give it all to you. She silently sobbed; she released all the pain, all the frustration, all the guilt that she felt.

*****

"Mama, are you ok?" Alexis patted Brenda on the shoulders. "You have been sitting here for like twenty minutes. It's time to go to church, right?" She asked with her other two sisters right behind her. Each held the babies.

"Yes, I'm okay, Lexi," she raised her head a bit; her face was still wet from the cleansing that had taken place. "I just had to have a talk with the Lawd. That's all. I feel much better now."

Sabrina and Alexis looked at each other, they questioned their mothers' behavior, before they could say anything, Brandy interrupted the silence and said, "God is good, God is great. Thank you, Lord, for our family. Amen."

Brenda silently cheered once, as her tears strolled down her eyelids again, but unlike her previous tears, they were tears of joy. For the Bible states that wisdom comes from the mouth of babes. Brandy was no baby, but she was the youngest of the three sisters, and that moment of her speaking up about God, made Brenda one of the proudest mother's alive.

"Mama, I need money for church, you know how them church folks be collecting money for every service." Sabrina giggled with her hand held out towards Brenda.

"This is not a charity, do I look like a charity case to you. I don't have any money, if you really want to put some money into the church, why don't you start by taking some of those nickels and dimes you have shoveled under your bed and put some of that in the collection basket."

"Mama, what happens if I don't have any money, will I get kicked out of the church?" Brandy asked, nervous about what the proper church manners were.

"No, sweetie." Brenda laughed; she knew that her lack of church attendance had also affected the girls in a negative way as well. "This is not the club. You don't have to pay an entrance fee to get into church, but as my mother loves to say, Jesus did have to pay a price for us to enter the kingdom of heaven."

"Oh. Wow. Maybe that's what I was dreaming about last night, some place called heaven. There were these huge puffed up clouds and people as far as I could see. And I saw like three rainbows, mommy. It seemed like such a peaceful place. It had to be heaven. I saw Angels, Mermaids and little boys in heaven. Heaven is where I want to be." Brandy said with her youthful cheer, all hopes for her were up. She knew that her dream was worth more than a dream. It was worth a possibility to explore exactly what heaven had to offer.

"Me too baby, me too. Heaven is also where I want to be. But you know what, in order for you to get to that magical place; you must first go to church. That's where we're going tonight; the church is where all the magic begins." Brenda smiled, and they each headed for the front door to make their way to the church.

Let the Church Say Amen

"Ladies and gentleman, we are living in a day and time when things aren't the way they used to be. We have wars and rumors of war. Crime rates at an all-time high, affordable health care is no longer affordable anymore, and the middle class has been squeezed near the brink of extinction.

Listen here church; this world has some issues. We have taken God out of the schools and God out of our homes. Some pastors have even taken God out of the church, or they will say God, but won't recognize Jesus. The word says that the way to the father is through the Son, and that's Christ Jesus. Jesus bled so that we can be set free. Our world is changing folks. You hear me, saints. Our world is changing. We have men loving men and women loving women and everybody seems to have a parade and think that. That's all right. But I come to tell you now. Our God is not pleased. He is not pleased with our wicked behavior."

Alexis cringed at the sound of Pastor Sanders reprimanding of women sleeping with women. In her mind, the moment she had with Sylvia was just a casual experiment; she felt that she couldn't have really been thinking about fully being a lesbian. Perhaps that was just a phase for her; she considered it as just an error of her youth. Whether it was a phase or not, the words Pastor Sanders spoke, still sent a dagger to her confused heart.

Brenda looked on intently at the pastor. She thought about her addictions, visions of the men she slept with swarmed her mind again. She could still smell the scent of her last beau's cologne. She could hear the bed rock, and the pleasurable moans she exhaled seeped deep down in her spirit. "Oh, my god," she silently blurted out.

Oooh, I know I'm a sinner. That boy was so good to me the other day, he nearly broke my back. We did use a condom, but if Ma finds out I'm pregnant again, she'll be sending me to more than church. She'll probably be sending me to the abortion clinic. Oh, Lord, I pray that his condom didn't slip off of him. I pray that he did not release his seed inside me. I have one mouth to feed, and he is getting big. Lord knows I can't afford to feed another, especially when I can barely feed myself.

Lord, please forgive me of my sins. I've been a real bad girl. Sabrina willed herself to focus back in on the preacher.

Brandy was silent, but she too was daydreaming. The rapture could have come and swept her up, but she wouldn't have known it. All she could think about was the Angels and boys, which filled her dream the prior night.

"Mommy, am I going to see an Angel today?" She lightly pulled on Brenda's coat pocket.

Brenda turned and gave her a look of utter disgust, the same type of look that her mother gave her when she spoke during the preaching of the word. "If the Lord God willing baby, we will see some Angel's right here in Square Pentecostal Church, ok. So you keep still now and listen to the pastor." She shook her head in disbelief. *I have to teach these girls some proper church manners.*

The Pastor continued. "Saints, if you will, please turn with me to Luke Chapter seven beginning with verse three and ending with verse eight, and the Scripture says... When the Centurion heard about Jesus, he sent to him elders of the Jews, asking him to come and heal his servant. And when they came to Jesus, they pleaded with him, earnestly saying, He is worthy to have you do this for him, for he loves our nation, and he is the one who built us our synagogue. And when Jesus went with them. When he was not far from the house, the centurion sent friends, saying to him, Lord do not trouble yourself for I am not worthy enough to have you come under my roof. Therefore, I did not presume to come to you. But say the word, and let my servant be healed." Pastor Saunders paused for a moment.

"Let the church say amen." Pastor looked around as he was jolted by a cheerful reply.

"Amen." The members of the church said in agreement, each one dressed casually for the Thursday night Bible study, everyone except Brenda's family. Brenda and the girls were dressed for Sunday service; this made them a target for the Pastor, as he constantly looked their way as he knew that they functioned as unfamiliar faces in a membership that served no more than a hundred strong and usually on

Thursday nights, the flock was normally thirty-
percent of that. Lucky for them, the church was not
well lit, so no one was able to fully make out their
faces. The only person that was afforded the bright
lights was the pastor behind the podium delivering
the word. Brenda wasn't thinking straight when she
had her daughters to dress in their Sunday best, since
she was a CME Christian, she was used to having
herself and her daughters wear the best whenever she
went to church on those special holidays.

    *Something about this pastor just don't sit well in
my spirit. He looks awfully familiar to me.* Brenda
thought to herself. *He looks like somebody I used to kick it
with back in the day. Aww...he's so handsome and he talks
so smooth. I really think I know this brotha.*

    "So as we find here in Luke, with the story of
the Centurion man, we find that... that a healing was
needed with this man. This Centurion man knew that
Jesus was the key, but he felt unworthy to be in his
presence. How many of you feel like this? How many
of you feel unworthy to be in the presence of the Lord
because of whatever sin you have committed? How
many of you know that a prayer delayed is not a
prayer denied?"

    Some of the church mothers moaned in
agreement, even waving their hands as a witness.

    "Church, this world, our lives is in a desperate
need of a healing, there is just too much sin going on
for us to keep doing the same thing and the same
thing all the time. But just like the Centurion man, we
are not worthy to be in the presence of the Lord, but

it's by His grace and mercy, by His stripes that we are healed saints. Do you hear me church, by His stripes, by the blood of Jesus that we are healed?"

The church roared with praise, giving thanks and worship to God. The church members could not be contained, but Brenda and the girls were not moved.

Brenda looked on at the pastor as she tried to put the pieces together; she tried hard to figure out where she had met such a handsome and well-spoken gentleman. He had to be around her age. He reminded her of one of her old flings. He reminded her so much of Malcolm. Malcolm had been one of the guys she met when she was running tricks for Michael Lewis, Malcolm was a regular. He was a young dude at the time no more than twenty and she was twenty-two.

Brenda never understood why Malcolm would volunteer to pay for a prostitute when he was so handsome with his thick wooly hair, deep brown eyes, and athletic build. She was partially in love with Malcolm. He was one of the only regulars who she felt any real emotion for, and otherwise, she was just going through the motions to get her few dollars and on to the next one. When she questioned Malcolm about his spending habits on her, he once said, "Paying a prostitute was cheaper than having a girlfriend because at least I know that every time I pull out this twenty, I'm guaranteed to score big. With a girlfriend, you have to wine and dine and not get any. That's just too much money for no thrills."

Malcolm's comment gave her the chills, but she knew all along that what he said was true, in some ways that made her want him even more, but she knew the boundaries that the business had, and dating your clients were one of the no no's in the rule book.

Malcolm stopped patronizing her after she became pregnant with Alexis, the second child she bore to Michael Lewis. In some ways, she wished that Malcolm was the father of her child, she loved him more than she had loved Michael, either way, no paternity test was done at the time, so her and Michael assumed that the baby were both of their doing considering the fact that he was the only guy she did not use protection with or so she could recall. Of course, she was hurt by Malcolm's departure, and so she bid in her heart that one day she would see him again.

"As I begin to close this Bible study, I would like for you to turn with me to Revelations chapter seven verse fifteen. The word of God reads like this…Therefore they are before the throne of God, and serve him all day and night in his temple; and he who sits on the throne will shelter them with his presence. They shall hunger no more, neither thirst anymore; the sun shall not strike them, or any scorching heat. For the Lamb in the midst of the throne will be their shepherd, and he will guide them to springs of living water, and God will wipe away every tear from their eyes. And let the church say--."

"Malcolm--Malcolm is that you, the one who used to come down Collins Avenue back in the day and kick it with me?" Brenda disrupted the service without a care in the world. The church groaned with their disapproval. Even Sabrina nudged her in her side. But Brenda was ecstatic; she just had a gut feeling that the pastor before her was her lover from the past.

Pastor Saunders looked on at Brenda, confused at her sudden outburst, for he thought everyone knew that his name was Pastor Malcolm Saunders, not only was it written on the board outside, but was also included in the program. Pastor Saunders' wife turned around and looked at Brenda with grave disapproval. If she could have had it her way like the old *Burger King* slogan, she would have got up and reprimanded Brenda for her outburst, then checked the facts on her allegations.

Who is this strange woman yelling out my husband's name in the middle of service?

"Yes, I am Pastor Malcolm Saunders, now if you please. I have a service to conclude. I can speak with you after the service." He looked away from Brenda; he focused his attention back on the book of Revelations. "Let the church say amen."

The church said, "Amen." He eyed Brenda cautiously and prayed that she wasn't going to have another outburst. But Brenda could not contain herself, the joy she felt for seeing one of her first true loves could not be contained. She decided to go to the restroom. On her way to the restroom, she made a split second change in plans and ended up pulling out a cigarette. She exited the church and lit it up, sat down on the steps of the church and smoked her cigarette right on the front steps of the church.

Malcolm up there talking about a healing, well I'm being healed right now. This tobacco does wonders to a sister girl's mind when under a lot of stress and excitement.

In the meantime, the pastor closed out his sermon a little weaker than normal. He could tell that the *amen's* and *yes sir's* did not come out from the congregation as strong as they had under normal circumstances, but Brenda's sudden outbreak was surely not a normal circumstance, and therefore, his anxious thoughts on meeting Brenda had taken him off the mind of the Lord. As he said the benediction, he noticed that Brenda still hadn't returned to her seat, the girls had disappeared, too.

Malcolm briskly walked to the back to do his normal hand shaking routine, his wife was near his side, and she noticed his anxiety.

"Malcolm, who is that woman who was talking about kicking it with you back in the day?" first lady Urethra had asked with a stressed demeanor.

"Baby, I don't know that woman." He kept shaking hands. He also saw the questioning expressions of the other saints. He knew he had to be careful because he knew that there was nothing more poisonous for a church than a gossiping church member.

"Let's talk about this at home, baby." He tried to calm his nerves, but the damage had already been done. The church wanted to know who the woman who intimately yelled his name was.

"Well, has she left already? Where is she?" Urethra looked around confused and shocked all at the same time.

"According to one of the deacons, she had already left, leaving a cigarette bud on the church steps." Malcolm said. He tried to calm his wife's nerves; he wanted to ease her of any tension that she may have felt.

"Well, whoever she is, she surely has no respect for the house of the Lord. These grounds are holy grounds. That means no smoking, no drinking, nothing on the grounds of the church."

"Honey, I know that, but does she know this as well? All the members of the church had exited the building and the only people that were left inside were Pastor Malcolm, his wife, two kids and one of the deacons, who was a key holder and worked security for the church.

"Pastor, we are all locked up, you and your wife are good to go."

"Thanks, Deacon. Come on, Urethra, let's go children." Pastor Malcolm did one more survey of the sanctuary, just in case Brenda and her kids were ducked behind the pews or something. He scratched his head as he tried to place the image of her in his mind to see if it would bring back any memories, but to his avail, the lightning of the church was darker than usual, so he didn't get a full opportunity to vest the image that was before him. Although her voice did sound familiar, it still wrecked his mind to pinpoint the woman who visited his church and dared to call his name with such intimate conviction before the presence of his wife.

Pastor Malcolm turned off the lights to the sanctuary and escorted his family outside the church and on their way home, it surely wasn't the Bible study that they were used to having, but then again, as the age-old saying suggested, *God works in mysterious ways.*

The Girl in the Yellow Skirt

I *can remember very vividly my junior year; there was this red boned honey full of finger licking goodness, walking down the hallway the first day of school that year. Of course, I was at Miami Carol City throughout my high school days and I never recalled seeing that chick. She must have been a transfer or something. But either way, besides that point, this girl was all the rage for me; I literally wanted to put her on a full-course platter, taking in each part of her one minute at a time. The chick had this bright yellow skirt that did a number on my senses. I mean she had me drooling like a dog panting for water.*

Her name was Bethany Brown; she had a nice smile, clever curves and the guys swarmed all over for her number. Bethany was one of the cutest, fanciest chicks I ever met at Carol City High. I wanted her number as bad as the dudes, and I'd do anything in the world just to get the seven digits.

Although Bethany Brown was a big highlight for me during my junior year, the biggest highlight was the fact that my baby girl, Kita, had turned one years old. It was a very proud moment for me, believe me. I didn't think that there was any way that I was going to make a full year of dirty pampers, nursing and sleepless nights, I was ready to put that girl up for adoption or something.

Sylvia and I had our off and on flings, but it was never to the point of our first time. In the best interest of our friendship, her and I had decided to take a break from our sexual desires, especially considering the fact that I was

constantly pulling away from her, ready to devour the next
chick, and torn by the lust I still felt for boys.

"You know, not every man can handle a chick
like me. I make the boys go wild and the girls get
stupid." Bethany Brown said, as her and Alexis
introduced each other.

"So--um--where are you from?" Alexis
stuttered, shocked, and amused that she finally had
the opportunity to meet and communicate with the
girl of her dreams.

"I'm from Charleston, South Carolina, and you,
my friend, stutter like the guys when they meet me. If
I didn't know any better, I'd think that you would be
trying to holla at me."

Alexis went into a nervous rage, with the fear
of rejection that loomed. She tried her best to smile,
and act normal, but the urges she felt for the girl in
the yellow skirt were powerfully intoxicating and
severely addicting.

"Hello--- answer me, are you deaf or
something, what's up with you, girl?" Bethany Brown
grew agitated with Alexis's mode of silence; it was as
if Alexis placed Bethany into a celebrity status, which
caused her feelings to go numb. Therefore, it gave
room to her lack of expression.

" I'm bout to bounce." Bethany grew tired of
the sudden weirdness; she clicked her keys, and stood
up, reached for her half-consumed cafeteria food to
throw away upon leaving the cafeteria.

"Hey, wait." Alexis thought quickly on her feet.
"I'm sorry, I just haven't met anyone as pretty as you

before. I also have never met anybody from South Carolina. In all honesty, I hardly meet anybody outside the projects." *I hope that works, this chick is too nice on the eyes to pass up on.*

Sensing the compassion in her voice, Bethany sat back down; she looked around at all the male faces that seemingly disapproved of her move. She could tell that they were silently booing inside; they wished they had taken the chance to escort her from the cafeteria when they had the split second opportunity to do so, for that moment, they just had to wait.

"Yeah, I was a military brat til' my parents just recently got divorced, my mother got a huge lump sum of money and decided to move me and my lil' brother down here like two weeks ago. There ain't much difference going on in Charleston, South Carolina, and Miami. I mean, we have beaches just like here; my daddy is still based at the Charleston Air force Base."

"Okay, cool, so like what do you like to do?" Alexis felt more comfortable.

"I like to chill at the beach, hang out at house parties with my girlfriends, and of course, make out with boys. What about you?" She questioned while eyeing her watch, and the petty cat calls from the surrounding guys.

"Well, I um--" Alexis was back to stuttering, but Bethany was not upset in the least by this. As a matter of fact, she seemed to be amused that a female was that nervous and shy around her, as she said, she was used to the guys acting as such.

Alexis noticed the smirk on Bethany's face and was slightly embarrassed. "I typically don't hang out much since I am a single mother; I have a lot of responsibilities. My baby is my first responsibility, especially since her daddy doesn't care much about her. Have you ever wondered, how could men, or shall I say little boys be so heartless, especially when it comes down to taking care of their own?"

"I feel you. I wish I had an answer to that, I'm sure that's like a topic on every female's mind. You see that boy over there?" Alexis turned around to see whom she was referencing. "That's Micah. He promised me some flowers and a movie tonight." Micah blew a kiss in their direction. Alexis was grossed out, but Bethany batted her eyes back at him.

Why is she looking at him when she should be paying attention to me? I'm the one at the table with her now, not him.

"You see, girl, it's all a part of a game to them. That boy don't care about me, I'm used to horny dudes like him from back home, but guys down here seem to be a little more aggressive. Okay-Okay check out dude to the left of us." Alexis slowly tilted her head to the left. She didn't want to be too obvious. "Well, that's Joseph. He promised to take me to the beach tomorrow." Unlike Micah, Joseph did not blow any kisses. He was more of the shy type, and had looked away when he noticed two of the most beautiful girls in the school at the time look his way.

Alexis pretended to be excited about Bethany's prospects, but the excitement was a mere façade to cover up the disappointment she felt.

"And check out the boy to the right of us, the football player. Girl, he told me that he'd get rid of his chick in a minute to be with me, and I can believe that. But once he done got what he wanted from me, he would get rid of me, too." The football player had no immediate action either, as he pretended to hold a decent conversation with his girlfriend and fellow teammates, but he did manage to wink his eye a split second at Bethany once his girlfriend reached in her purse for her makeup.

"Enough about all these guys, are you dating anybody?" Bethany asked with a doubtful demeanor, she wasn't sure what to expect from that question as their lunchtime was winding down.

Alexis blurted out the political answer, while she tightly masked her true feelings in fear of being either hurt or rejected. "No, I'm not dating anyone right now, as stated before I'm always on mommy duty. I wish I could go out places, but it is what it is. I love my baby though, wouldn't trade that girl for nothing in the world."

Bethany felt bad for Alexis, so she decided to invite her to a house party hosted by her new friend. "Hey, um--um, my friend and I are throwing this party at her house tonight. I would really like for you to come if you can. It's a really different kind of party than you've *probably* experienced. My friends and I up in Charleston used to host these types of parties all the time. I think that you'll have a lot of fun." She smiled. Not a minute after, the bell had rung.

Alexis thought hard through all the sudden commotion, she knew it was her turn to babysit her nephew and dreaded the favor she would have to ask of Sabrina, who was on schedule to work later that night. "Well, I have to think about it, here is my number, can you shoot me a text of the address just in case I'm able to go."

"Sure, I'll do that when I get to class. Bye."

Alexis hoped that the party could potentially be an opportunity to score even more one on one time with Bethany Brown, but she knew that the competition would be fierce as there was a huge possibility that the same guys Bethany was pointing at in the cafeteria, would be the same guys who showed up to the party. Alexis took to caution in her observation of Bethany in her yellow skirt, with her pink diamond earrings, cross-shaped belt buckle and legs that reminded her of another beautiful celebrity. Indeed, Bethany Brown was one of the finest girls to arrive at Miami Carol Senior High, but Alexis was ready, even if it meant an all-out war with the boys.

*****

Alexis convinced Sabrina to stay home from work and borrowed her old beaten up '92 Chrysler Plymouth that was purchased for four-hundred dollars from a junkyard.

Alexis was a block away from the address of the house party. It was located in the Kendall area, which was approximately twenty minutes south of where Alexis lived. Of course, Sabrina gave Alexis a big fuss, til' Alexis decided to pay her wages for the day, which was a total of fifty-dollars, and convinced Sabrina to call in sick to work. She bartered her food stamps in order to get the fifty, the same crime she accused her mother of, she did. She expressed to Sabrina why that particular house party was very important to her, which was how she earned her sisters' beaten up car. Of course, she left out the details that she had a crush on Bethany Brown.

When she arrived near the house, there were cars lined up throughout the street, Alexis was happy to park Sabrina's car half a block down, she did not want anyone else to see her clunker, she tightened up her hair, took another peek in the mirror, then walked towards the mansion.

"Wow, this is a huge house," Alexis said under her breath as her excitement built. She saw all sorts of fancy cars lined through the street and neighbor's driveways, there were cars she couldn't imagine pronouncing and was sure to never have heard of them before.

As she grew closer and closer to the house, she began to see more and more familiar faces, she saw Sylvia, Monique, and Claritha, but no real sign of Bethany anywhere.

"Hey, ladies." Alexis forced herself to speak to her fair weathered friends as they each were just a few feet away from the entrance of the house.

Claritha chimed in. She looked at Alexis suspiciously. "Well, I didn't know that you attended these types of parties?" She braced for impact.

"What are you talking about? What type of party? I received an invite from Bethany, so here I am."

Sylvia and Monique giggled like two little girls eating ice cream.

"Oh, so you don't know?" Claritha looked Alexis up and down; she could not resist the urge to tell Alexis what was really going on. "Don't you notice something strange about all these groups of girls going in at a time, where are the men?"

"I've been to house parties before; everyone knows that the men don't show up til' an hour after the women." Alexis felt a tingle in her chest, her so-called friends were acting very strange. She wanted to pull Sylvia to the side to get the details, but then again, that would have made her look too suspicious. So she decided to just catch her breath and play along with Claritha's relentless effort to taunt her.

"Well, if you don't know, chick, you sure as heck about to find out." They were only one step away from entering the home, when suddenly, a huge set of eyes all shifted towards one direction. "Oh, my gosh." Alexis couldn't believe her eyes.

The two matriarchs of the party had arrived in a white stretched C-300 Bentley Limousine. The middle-aged Hispanic driver went around to the passenger side and opened the door, before anyone saw who it was, there was a long loose knit yellow dress, made for Cinderella, and it sparkled with an array of costume jewelry, while her neckline glittered with gold, as she was fully outside the car. Her smooth rich buttermilk skin was perfectly crafted with a blend of dark chocolate. It was Bethany. She walked the red carpet with a strut and style unknown to most girls in the south; she proudly expressed each feature that her white father and black mother put together. She waved at the group of ladies like a star, as they each had their camera phones snapping away at such an array of beauty and grace.

Her friend stepped out of the limo with a dark black dress that looked a little too loose for her. She did not have the same sort of reception, although she too walked the red carpet, few phones were out to capture her special moment. In their world, there was only one queen, and Bethany was definitely the 'Queen B' as the handful of girls followed her into the wonderfully sophisticated and decorated home, fit for a celebrity.

After Bethany's co-host entered the house, the rest of the girls joined in, in what would be the official start to their house party. Alexis looked around the house and became suspicious of all the girls who were there, and then with a moment's flash, she saw a few girls in the back corner making out. First, she just blew it off as just an isolated incident. Then, with a closer look around there were girls making out on the sofa, around the pool, girls playing around with adult toys. She suddenly felt a tinge of discomfort, although she slightly enjoyed the atmosphere, she hoped that one of her friends could come to her rescue.

"Now do you see what I'm talking about?" Claritha jumped at the chance to explain why she questioned Alexis before they gathered inside the house.

"Well, I see lots of girls, but I'm sure the guys will be coming soon," she said nervously, she wanted to make sure that Claritha knew that she still had her *straight* card intact. But her experiments with Sylvia could have been leaked out to Claritha, although Sylvia had promised her to secrecy.

Claritha laughed, "You are so naïve, there are no men coming to this party tonight. You see your little friend over there passing a wet kiss on the lips of her home girl?" Claritha pointed in Bethany's direction. Alexis gasped. She couldn't believe her eyes.

"Never say I didn't tell you so, so get with the program or leave. No one needs a party pooper."

Sylvia could not take another moment of Claritha's disrespect of her best friend. "Leave the girl alone, Claritha. She just came to have fun. She didn't know that this was an all girls' party. Chill out, go get some Kool-Aid or something, I heard that it's spiked anyway." Claritha left. She turned around and twisted her hips hard so everyone could notice the direction she was headed in. That's one thing about being in an all-girls party, they had to either do something spectacular or awkwardly dumb to get the other female's attention, otherwise they were just another girl in the number.

"Are you ok, girl? I'm sure that this is probably not what you were expecting, right?" Sylvia tried her best to comfort Alexis.

"No, not at all, but I'm cool though." She lied. She wondered what the girls at school would think of her, and since she had attended the all girl's party, even worst she wondered would happen if her mother and sisters found out.

"Okay, but you know I see you eyeing that broad over there." Sylvia chuckled a bit.

"Who are you talking about?" she questioned; she hoped her secret crush on Bethany was not that obvious.

Sylvia responded with a look of displeasure. "Stop trying to act dumb, you know who I am talking about, if you have feelings for Bethany, why don't you gone on over there and talk to her, unless you just want to continue to see the potential girl of your dreams make out with that whore that is not even close to your level of beauty and perfection. Stop trying to act like you all the way straight, girl, nobody cares in here what you are, the majority of the girls are bi-sexual." She took a quick sip of the spiked Kool-Aid, and then went off on a nervous giggle.

Dang, am I that obvious with my feelings that Sylvia could see right through me. So-what if I like Bethany, I hope that Sylvia ain't trying pull the jealousy card.   "Why do you think Bethany hangs out with all those dudes in school, and she's the new girl, too? Bethany ain't giving those guys no play, at least that's what I heard. That's all a front for what she really is, and to say it plain and simple, the girl is a dike. And one fine dike for sure."

Alexis smiled. She couldn't contain the thoughts of pleasure she felt for Bethany. She wished at that moment that she were strung around Bethany's arms, dancing around the floor, whispering sweet nothings to each other, but she knew that it was all a dream, and unless something happened, in reality, all dreams had to come to an end.

"So what's up with you and Monique?" Alexis broke the ice, clearly there was something that Sylvia did not tell her between the two friends.

"There ain't nothing going on between Monique and I, it's Claritha and I that like to spend a few times underneath the sheets. I'm still straight, girl, don't worry about that, I just seem to gravitate to women better, especially since they seem to better understand my emotional and spiritual needs ten times better than men. All men want to do is pierce you with their little sword and go to sleep on top of you. You know how you and I were when we reached both our physical and spiritual climax. We were in heaven."

"Alexis, it was good seeing you. I have to run, booty. I mean duty is calling." Claritha signaled for her presence. "I believe that Claritha found a room for us to hide out in, go get your girl, Alexis."

"Ok, Sylvia. Bye." Monique followed behind Sylvia and Claritha.

I guess three is company. Alexis thought to herself, she did not want to think about her friends anymore. It was time for her to go for the kill shot. Bethany was briefly free from company, just the break she needed, and it was confession time.

Just as Alexis lingered over in Bethany's direction, another girl ceased the moment and stepped right in front of Alexis, Alexis couldn't bear to be hurt, she was ready to fight, she was a project chick, and the little white suburban girl was about to feel her wrath.

"Hold up one second, I believe that this girl here wanted to talk to me first," Bethany intervened. She noticed the grim look and balled up fist that accompanied Alexis' demeanor. Relieved by the momentary intervention, her blood began to flow back naturally and her willingness to fight had subsided. Bethany had winked at her, so Alexis made her way up the marble stairs.

I hope I am making the right choice. Alexis nervously thought.

"Hey, glad you can make it, are you enjoying yourself so far?" Bethany asked, she made small talk as she eyed the long line of girls who wanted to talk to her.

"Yeah, I'm good. This is definitely not what I was expecting." Alexis admitted.

"Well, what were you expecting?" Bethany moved her head closer to Alexis so she could hear her better.

"Well, I kind of was expecting some guys to be here. That's all." She hoped that she did not sound too forward or ungrateful for the invite.

Bethany decided to play around with her a bit. "So, wait a minute. You don't think that I'm pretty?"

"No. That's not what I am saying; I think that you are a very pretty girl." She said softly while she looked away.

"For someone who was pretty mad a few seconds a go, you seem to be pretty shy to me. But I knew that you were crushing on me when we were in the cafeteria earlier today. Are you digging what you see?" Bethany was bold in her questioning; she'd rather get to the point than leave the truth hanging out there on a scavenger hunt waiting to be found.

"Yeah, like I said, you are pretty and all."

"But do you want to kiss me?" Bethany pushed.

"Yeah, I guess. I think I want to kiss you." *I know I want to kiss her. Her lips are only half an inch from mine now. This is definitely too good to be true.*

Bethany eased back a bit. "Well, you will have to wait in line like the rest of these chicks."

And just like a ton of bricks falling one-hundred feet from the sky, so did the weight of hearing that particular news from Bethany, Alexis was torn, hurt beyond relief. She immediately ran outside swearing and all. She did not stop running til' she met the first element of her real life, her sister's ugly beat up car. But no matter how she felt about that car. She'd rather endure the shame in driving that car around town than the shame she felt in being rejected by her first true crush on another woman.

Sure, what she and Sylvia had done was experimental and they had genuine feelings for each other as best friends. But Bethany was the type of woman who Alexis had been waiting for all along, and the rejection she felt from Bethany was too harsh for her to even comprehend correctly.

My Chick Bad

The day that followed Alexis's crushed heart, was a pretty hard day for Alexis at Carol City High, the feel and smell of being rejected was still fresh on her heart, as she had cold-stone feelings for her fellow peer. Alexis was madly depressed, and a moment of silence was all she wanted, but could not get it with all the girls who chimed in on the party, calling it, 'the party of the century.'

This is not fair, life is not fair, and why could you never get the one that you like the most. I stepped out on the limb for this, I risked people calling me gay, all to get rejected and looked at like a fool in front of Bethany. I hope that Sabrina does not find out about my feminine attractions. I'm sure she'll be putting her two cents in.

"Hey, girl, how you doing?" Bethany asked Alexis in passing as if nothing had ever happened between them on the prior night. Well, technically, nothing happened. But for Alexis, everything happened for her. All of her pent up emotions, all of her loose feelings, were all expressed that one night, a night that may have indeed changed her life forever.

She didn't want to show any signs of weakness or pain in her heart, Alexis spoke, but with a hurried tone. "Hey, Bethany, I'm kind of running late for class, but good to see you, nice party last night." Alexis scurried off; she didn't want to hear any rebuttal from Bethany.

"Ok. Bye," Bethany clicked her teeth. *If she only knew...* And just like that, she disappeared into the hallway; she headed into the opposite direction of Alexis.

Once Alexis felt that she was in a comfortable space away from Bethany, she glanced back, all to see just a small shadow of the woman her heart quickly felt for. And as if she was on cue for a stage play, she quietly whimpered to herself. She hoped that she could find some sort of solace in the confusion she felt. *Is my attraction for woman worth this type of heartache, is it worth this type of rejection? This here feels worse than my relationship with Ricky. Maybe with time, this will all make sense. Maybe I should just be with dudes. I don't know. I'm hellishly confused.*

*****

"How was the party last night, Lexi?" Sabrina inquired.

"Shh...mom could be listening; you know how she done got all religious on us lately."

"Yeah, you got a point, so how was the party?" She asked as softly as her baby slept. "Was it worth paying me to take off work? I mean, I've never seen you so excited about something before, at least not in a long time. So...who's the lucky guy who has taken all of your attention, I bet he's probably the cutest thing you've ever seen since Ricky. Did he kiss you, and you gave him the digits, right?" Sabrina noticed that she was doing more talking than waiting for a response from Alexis; so she decided to pause for a moment to give Alexis an opportunity to speak. Alexis looked dumbfounded as if she was unaware that naturally it was her time to speak since Sabrina had given her the floor.

Alexis began with the first few lies. "Well--um---it's not a guy, I just was so excited to be in attendance at one of the biggest parties of the school year." She wanted nothing more than to take a hot shower, lathered in the perfect perfumes and dyes. She was a nervous wreck.

"How come you didn't invite me silly? I would have had mama and Brandy to watch these babies. You never invite me to stuff." Sabrina had put up a childish fit.

"You're not in high school anymore, Sabrina, by the way, aren't you going to Miami-Dade Community College next semester? Why would you want to be around a bunch of high school twits? You grown up now, gurl." Alexis managed to laugh, even through the heavy feelings of guilt that were eating up at her core.

"Listen, chick, I just graduated only like a year ago. It's not like I'm trying to be some kind of sexual predator or something. I just hate this regular routine these days. It's boring. I mean I go to work, watch the kids, and play mama's numbers and sit around watching television. It's like my social life has gone to zero."

Sabrina exposed all of her insecurities, "I have no friends, no life. Uh--life sucks. Why couldn't I have just kept my legs closed and my prayers open? I wouldn't be in this mess. Don't get me wrong, I love my son. He's the cutest thing. God's gift to me, but I feel like I just kind of like had him too young." She shook her head in silence. She thought about all the stress that seemed to mount daily; she was in a desperate need to break the normal cycle of her life.

"Let's not forget that you have another one on the way, Sabrina. How could you go to some party with another baby moving and kicking in your stomach?"

That reality check set Sabrina off.

"So--- I don't want this baby. I already have one, why do you have to bring that up in my face as if I don't know? I'm already four and a half months through. I did everything I could to protect myself from this, but look at me!" She furiously pointed at her stomach. Neither one of them noticed that Brenda had crept into the kitchen to figure out what was all the commotion going on in her house.

"You did everything but tried out celibacy. Yeah, it's my fault though; I wasn't a good example to you gals with all the men I had running through here all times of the night. So I am the one to blame for baby number two. I---I just don't know how we are going to do it. It's already a struggle now. Something has to give. I just wish that the good Lord will cause some sort of financial breakthrough to happen for us. This is bad." She shook her head, and left, all to briefly return just as quickly as she had left.

"Girls, get ready for church, we are going back to that Pastor Saunders church. I believe that I know him, I believe I know him real well, especially if that is the Malcolm Saunders I knew back in the day." She grinned.

"Mama, how come you never told us about him, you never wanted to talk about that loud outburst you made in the church three months ago. I hope you don't embarrass us again." Sabrina scolded her.

I'd rather go to the raggedy old church down the street that we been going to every other Sunday than to have to go there. Sabrina thought to herself.

Brenda apparently was not listening, for if she was, she would have backhanded Sabrina faster than one could say 'Santa'. Truly that would have been a gift to the face that Sabrina would have rather not received, and fortunate for her, she did not receive it. Brenda reminisced once more on her times with Malcolm Saunders, her true first love. She was embarrassed about the outburst.

Alexis and Sabrina left the kitchen to take a shower and get dressed for church. Church for the two of them was the misery of their lives, but their younger sister Brandy enjoyed every bit of it. Brenda had often said that Brandy would be the one that broke the Carter curse, she knew in her heart that Brandy would be the one to stay pure and seek a relationship the right way, one that was applicable towards marriage and the sanctity of the marriage bed being undefiled. But Brenda also knew that in order for Brandy to break the curse, she herself had to let loose some men who were knocking on her bedroom door.

I just wish that my babies and I could get it together, Lord; I know I haven't been right. That's a guarantee. But Lord, I'm praying for some answers. We are struggling, and we need you now more than ever. I know I have to get rid of the men, the drinking, the gambling, and cigarettes. I know this Lawd, but the temptation is so hard that I can't will myself to be the role model that I need to be for my babies and grandbabies. I guess I'm just gone have to give it all to you.

Brenda was drained, as she thought about the improvements, she had made with her relationship with God, but was also disappointed in the setbacks that still scarred her. *Maybe one day, I'll fully get it together, Lawd, hopefully that one day won't be too late.*

*****

It was a Sunday morning, the first Sunday morning of the month at Square Pentecostal Church, unlike the Thursday night Bible study the Carter family attended months prior. This particular Sunday morning service was packed with beautifully arrayed black people and a few whites sprinkled throughout the church. But it wasn't the color of the people that mattered in that church; it was the colors of what the saints had on that really caught the glimmering eyes of Brenda, Sabrina, and Alexis. Out of all the churches, they had attended, never before had they seen such a selection of purple, pink, yellow, and orange, and it wasn't even Easter Sunday.

"Ma, look at her, she looks like a Christmas ornament. Is it Christmas time already?" Brandy asked with an open smile.

"No, baby, of course, it's not Christmas time yet," Brenda replied with a smile of her own.

Meanwhile, Brenda could not believe her eyes. She felt so uncomfortable, and she knew she dressed her daughters in their Sunday best, but when she looked around the church, she realized that their best was not good enough. Her heart sank; never had she felt that bad in church. It was worse than her previous outburst. *Lawd, if dressing fine is another requirement to get to heaven, then my daughters and I are on our way to hell.*

"Good morning, church. I said good morning, church." Pastor Saunders energetically said in the microphone while he headed to the podium. A distraction of another kind was brewing in the back of the church, but the Pastor was too busy hyping the church up. He did not notice the small commotion and chatter that seemed to raise an octave as a certain individual began to pass the pews.

Upon arriving to the podium, Pastor Saunders put on his fake reading glasses, he claimed that the glasses made him look more spiritual, and they had nearly fell off his face at the sight of the young lady who was pressing closer to the front of the church. He even stuttered a little, and if it weren't for his fast twitch muscles, he would have dropped the microphone.

Embarrassed by her husband's response, Urethra Saunders turned around to see exactly what was going on in the back of the church; she secretly hoped that it wasn't Brenda stirring things up again. *If that lady is in our church causing some mess again, I'm gone lose my religion.* It wasn't Brenda; Brenda was comfortably seated in the fourth row to the left with her daughters. She was busy jogging her memories of her and Pastor Saunders. Brandy was drawing stick figures. Sabrina was texting her boyfriend and Alexis had her head swiveled to the back like the majority of the church folks, she adored the beauty that was almost near the front row. It was Bethany Brown.

Bethany was laced in some of the finest, sophisticated, and expensive clothing from head to toe. In her walk down the church aisle for her red carpet moment, her feet were nicely supported by pink and black trimmed *Jimmy Choo's*, the shoes of the stars. She wore a pink *Donna Morgan* strapless dress. Her neckline was engulfed with some of the prettiest pearls and she carried a thousand dollar multicolored *Burberry* handbag just for giggles. She made her way to her seat in the front row. The church members were still chattering as they were unanimously picking her as the unofficial winner for best dressed.

Dang....My Chick Bad. Well, my soon to be chick. She hurt my feelings real bad at the party though, I'm not sure if I'll be able to trust her. Alexis thought to herself, as her eyes discreetly followed Bethany all the way to her seat. Of course, her mother and sisters weren't paying much attention to Alexis; they too were in awe of the flawless beauty that just took everyone's attention from their real purpose of being in church, God.

Pastor Saunders caught his breath and pleaded for the church's attention. He figured a quick Scripture wouldn't work as he was originally set to read the book of Matthew chapter thirteen, which described the parable of the sower, so instead he went off program and had the choir to deliver a hymn.

"Well, I'll be darned; this young heffa done took my husband's attention up in this here church, now I have two women to compete with. Lord, help me. Being a pastor's wife is a tough thing, there is just too much competition for my man." Urethra stated under her breath, no one would have ever known, as it looked like she was just worshipping the Lord in song like the rest of the members. She was waving her hands smiling at the people, but deep inside, she began to harbor a certain hate for the two women who took her husband's attention. *Lord, please forgive me for calling that child a heffa, and help me, Lord, to not harbor any malice towards her or that Brenda chick.*

Urethra didn't take notice of Pastor Saunders lengthy gaze at Alexis. A look of confusion filled the bulb of both of his eyes, but just as he was about to go into depth with his thoughts, he shrugged them off and tuned his body around so that he could be glued in on the beautiful notes sung by the choir.

Urethra knew that a good man was hard to find, and having being raised in the projects herself, her story may have been a mirror of the type of narrative that had played out in the lives of Alexis and Sabrina. She grew up without a father and watched men treat her mother like a dog. But Urethra chose a different path in life. She decided to put herself head first in the books and to be a kept woman, she felt that as a girl out of the projects, the only true power that she had, was the power to be disciplined and maintain a sense of self-control. And with that great power, she stayed a virgin all the way through college, which was primarily funded by scholarships, government grants and a few student loans.

She kept her purity til' the time she met Malcolm at the mature age of twenty-six, and he was twenty-eight at the time. Malcolm was not a pastor when the two had met; he was a pastor in training. But like any man his age, his hormones were kicking and his drive for sexual innuendos did not decrease because of his title, in some ways his desires actually increased according to him. It served as a testing ground of his faith towards God and his own ability to put away the things of the flesh. He understood firsthand that there would be no sexual contact til' he and Urethra were married. That was made perfectly clear by her on their first date.

The two burned with passion for each other like a lamp with unlimited oil. They couldn't contain the feelings they harbored for the other, so they did what First Corinthians chapter seven and nine stated, 'It's better to marry than to burn with passion.' And so they married, Urethra gave Malcolm a part of her power, but only because the two had become one and she kept herself faithful to God through their wedding day.

They had two little boys and an opening came for Malcolm to preach at Square Pentecostal church just two years after they eloped.

Malcolm was the only man who Urethra had been with, and Urethra was the only woman who Malcolm had been with since they were engaged, and to Urethra's point, she intended on keeping it that way.

Caught Red Handed

"**D**id you see how hard Pastor Saunders was looking at you, Alexis?" Sabrina remarked with a glaze in her eyes and worry in her heart.

"What are you talking about? Pastor Saunders is a respectable pastor, with a beautiful wife and kids." *Not that his attraction would matter much to me, he looks good, but not my type.*

"I'm just saying, he was looking mighty hard at you. You feel me? He just looked kind of suspect, and I mean, it wasn't really like a look of him trying to holler at you or something, but more like....well....I don't know. Let me shut up." Sabrina backed off, she wasn't sure about what she felt, but she felt that something was up, something was going on that was out of the ordinary.

"We always seem to have these serious conversations here in the kitchen. You know that mama got ears longer than that hallway," Alexis remarked sarcastically.

Sabrina grinned, but deep inside, she just didn't feel herself, and with her baby kicking for her attention, she decided to sit down for a moment.

"Yeah, you right about moms, but I definitely think you wrong about that pastor Saunders cat. Anyway, I got somewhere to be in a few minutes, so if you don't mind keeping watch over Kita while I'm gone, I'd really appreciate that."

"Yeah, I'm sure you would. Have me here with the babies; while mama and Brandy go to the grocery store soon, so now everybody gone leave me here by myself. That's okay though, I'll do that for you." She paused after another kick. "You owe me one though. Where are you going anyway?" She looked down at her stomach, her baby shifted to the left a bit. *I promise, this is my last baby.*

"I'm bout to go chill with Sylvia for a minute, she's going to do my nails, and we'll probably watch some movies." Alexis did an about face and headed for the shower. But like the sister that Sabrina was, Sabrina had more to say.

"Well, it seems like you spend a mighty time with that Sylvia chick, you rarely even talk about Ricky any more. Well—heck." Alexis stopped her midsentence.

"There is no need for me to even talk about Ricky, you know how bad he's done me wrong, so— there really is no need for me to even spew him out of my mouth." She shook her head in frustration.

Sabrina blew off Alexis' statement as if she didn't even say it, she continued to speak her own opinions. "You barely even talk about men folk period. I remember times you and I used to be snuggled up in the room talking about the cutest guys in school. You remember, Rock, right?"

Alexis scanned her brain, as she turned around to face an annoyingly nosey Sabrina. "Yeah…kind of." she lied.

"Yeah, Rock, was that boy you used to always talk about, you know, the light skinned dude with braces on, you said that he was a geek, but he was pretty cute and all. I can't believe that you don't remember Rock from like two years ago. Didn't he try to get with you?"

Alexis remembered, but she didn't have time to talk about spoiled milk, especially since her window of time to meet Sylvia was winding down, so she brushed it off and went on her way to the bathroom to take a hot and steamy shower.

I don't know what's wrong with me, why am I so attracted to girls all of a sudden? Rock was cute, but he wasn't really my pace at the time. I don't know, Lord; I've been a bad girl lately. But I don't understand what's wrong with me having feelings for girls. If you say that you knew me before I was born, then you obviously knew that I was born this way. I don't know, church ain't helping either, maybe men will satisfy me again; just maybe a man will be what I want. But for now, I will do me.

*****

"I thought you weren't coming." Sylvia said with an apprehensive look on her face.

Alexis was breathless. "Yeah, my sister was drilling me like a general. You gone let me in?" Alexis questioned at the footsteps of Sylvia's door.

"Yeah sure, I'm just a little leery about this; my parents will be home soon." She signaled for Alexis to enter.

"I thought you said they didn't get home til' six in the evening. Why you tripping? That's two hours from now." She pouted.

"I know, Lexi, but I was planning on doing your nails first, then like, you know do our thing."

"That's crazy, first of all nails take a good minute to dry, then secondly, we can do our thang first, then get my nails did. That gives us perfect time before your people's get home." *I just prayed about this, and I'm not even trying to fight this. So why go to God anyway, to feel guilty. Sin is sin no matter how it's looked at, whether I'm banging a hot chick or screwing some dude. It's all sin; I just have to manage to get God out my head when I'm ready to do it. I hate this guilt part. Why can't God just leave me alone? Why can't He just go bother somebody on another planet or something?*

Sylvia relaxed a bit, as she nodded in agreement to Alexis's plan, she escorted her to her bedroom, it had been a while since the two had been together physically, and each of their estrogen levels soared, as their individual fragrances grew stronger on their nostrils. Before they even made it through the door, Alexis had slipped Sylvia a kiss on the cheeks. That was the kiss that set the tone for the rest of their affair.

Sylvia was breathing heavy; she was still confused about the time. "So what you want to do first?"

Alexis took it upon herself to take one of their favorite videos from under Sylvia's bed." Now you know how this video gets me in the mood." She

placed the video in the DVD player, as the girls
decided to waste no time undressing each other, they
revealed the pride of their mother's womb and the
sculpture of their nakedness. Neither questioned their
choice, for they had already grew deeper than they
ever had been in the lifestyle.

Sylvia playfully pushed Alexis to the bed as
she grabbed the remote to turn the volume up.

"Stop it." Alexis called, as she waited for her
best friend to let go of the remote and put her on play.

Right on cue, Sylvia let go of the remote as she
moaned for pleasure. Alexis took her legs and put
Sylvia into a lock. Sylvia's breast immediately perked
up a bit, and all the fears of her parents coming home
were quickly drowned out in the lust and passion she
felt for Alexis.

*****

"Sylvia---Sylvia where are you sweetie?"
Sylvia's mother had gotten off work an hour early,
after she suffered from a strong headache, the boss let
her take an hour's sick time.

She wanted nothing more to do than to find
her bed; Sylvia's mother was worried when Sylvia did
not respond, she knew her husband wouldn't be
home til' six in the evening, the same time she would
have normally been home as well. She knew that
somebody was in the house because the alarm system
was off, and she saw Sylvia's nail polish kit laid out
on the floor.

"Maybe that girl left and went to one of her friend's houses for the moment." She was nervous, and her head pounded even harder as she thought of some stranger walking around in their house unannounced. Even when Sylvia had went just a few blocks down the street. She still set the alarm. Instantly Sylvia's mother knew that something was wrong, but her headache did not allow her to think clearly, she walked in the kitchen and surfed through the mail, she decided to wait in the living room for her husband or Sylvia's arrival. But then there was a bump. The letters flew out of her hand, the four-hundred dollar light bill was shock enough, but with that bump, she was scared.

Just as she took a restless breath, there was another bump. "What in the world?" She turned around flabbergasted, her heart was beating heavy, and her forehead welcomed the sweat that released from every pore.

She finally realized that the bump had come from Sylvia's room. She figured that Sylvia couldn't have been home because she did not hear Sylvia's cell phone when she called it seconds prior. Afraid for what could have been waiting for her in Sylvia's room, she sent a quick text to her husband, picked up the broom from the kitchen and at a snail's pace; she headed down the long stretched hallway towards Sylvia's room.

As she got closer to Sylvia's door she noticed that the bumps became louder, more distinct, she would even hear voices. It was the sound of sex. She knew that her daughter was a teenager, and boys were always eyeing her daughter on a daily basis. She knew that she taught her daughter safe sex, but the scene she was about to witness was nothing she had spoken to her daughter about, nor was she remotely prepared for.

With another gulp of air and a shake of the head, Sylvia's mother opened the door. The door stretched wide open; she tip toed in and received the shock of her life. The grip she had on her broom was released instantly as it fell to the floor. She witnessed a bare light-skinned bottom tossing up and down in a rhythm that was ungodly. But the bareback bottom was not her daughter's bottom, it was Alexis, grinding and gyrating on top of a screaming Sylvia, as the wooden frame of the headboards were making the bumping sounds even more intense.

Oh, my Lord, what in the world is going in here? She was barely able to hold her composure, if it wasn't for her being able to get an immediate grip on the television stand, she would have fell backwards.

Neither girl had noticed Sylvia's mother enter into the bedroom; tears had released the grip of fear, as she secretly wished in her mind that it was a guy who Sylvia had been caught with. At least if it was a guy, she could have whipped the boy on site and sent him on his way. But a girl, she just didn't know how to handle it.

"Sylvia, what in the name of Jesus Christ is going on in here?" She screamed to the top of her lungs as she pushed the power button on the television.

The two girls were quickly startled, as they jumped out of the bed and looked for their clothes like Adam and Eve when they committed the great fall.

"Mamma-----it's not what you think." Sylvia said as she tightened her navy blue loose fit jeans.

Alexis backed away from the conversation. She still worked on pulling up her panties, she was scared and afraid at the same time. All that crossed her mind was what would be her family's reaction to the news that she was a Lesbian. But of course, she hated that label; she felt that Lesbian put her into a box, especially since she also had attractions for men. Pandora's Box was fully opened, and there was no hiding who she really was, she couldn't seem to control the desires of her heart.

Alexis loved the ecstasy of a woman, and no man was going to hold her back from that, even if it meant for her to be caught red handed.

Part 2

"Do you not know that the unrighteous will not inherit the kingdom of God? Do not be deceived. Neither fornicators, nor idolaters, nor adulterers, nor homosexuals, nor sodomites, nor thieves, nor covetous, nor drunkards, nor revilers, nor extortioners will inherit the kingdom of God."

1 Corinthians 6:9-10

The Hangover

I *wished that. That moment with Sylvia had not*
happened the way it did, but of course, it happened.
Memories of my mother and sister's reactions continue
to flash before my very eyes. Reminiscing on the verbal
lashing my mother gave me was enough to make me think
different about myself, but wasn't quite enough for me to
change the condition of my lifestyle choices. My mother
tried her best to keep me in solidarity from my sisters,
although my sisters embraced me with the kind of love that
anyone would want from their siblings, things between us
still were different, especially with Brenda trying to be top
cop in the house. It was just awful. She always kept tabs on
me when I was in the house, and she tried her hardest for
me not to interact with Brandy, I guess she feared my
lesbianism would magically rub off on her, she knew that
Sabrina could hold her own, but overall she treated me
different.

She treated me like an unwanted pet; I probably
would have felt more love at the pound. Her love was cold
and morbid, even under her religious disguise. She even
decided to put my baby, Kita, up for adoption. Brenda said
that I was unfit to be a mother with a lust after woman, she
was afraid that I would abuse my own child, although she
saw no such thing occur. She just went crazy. And at the
tender age of seventeen at that time, I had no choice but to
follow her wishes.

I really wished that Sylvia's mom didn't tell, I wish that she could have just kept the dirt between Sylvia and I our little secret.

"Hey, Lexi. snap out of it, you just chucked up everything you ate. What are you thinking about anyway?" A startled Karen asked as she witnessed a slightly slumped over Alexis who had fallen asleep on the toilet. "Girl, it's five in the morning, I thought you could hold your liquor."

With traces of old wet food inched around her mouth, Alexis reacted,

"Yeah, I said that I can hold my liquor." she passionately slurred her words like a good drunk. "But I didn't say that I could hold those wings and pizza down at the same time."

Karen laughed.

"Alexis when I came into this bathroom, you were in a complete daze, hugging the toilet like it was your favorite Teddy Bear. But---you looked like you were in some kind of deep thought as well. That part I didn't get."

"If you must know, I was thinking about the first time my mom and siblings found out that I was a Lesbian."

"Wasn't that like five years ago?" Karen shook her head.

"Yeah, I know, I just can't seem to get over those memories, those were some hard times for me at seventeen. I hated my mother, this lifestyle, and myself. It broke me Karen, it really broke me." A tear slid down her face, and then like a corkscrew pop of champagne the floodgates opened.

Her tears weren't the only gates that were being pressured to open; she moved her hands from around the base of the toilet. She slowly placed both hands on top of the toilet seat, and then she pressed down hard on the toilet seat while she lifted her body upright at the same time. She stumbled because she still was a little nauseous in the stomach; so she up chucked another round of fried chicken wings and pepperoni. That time she partially missed the toilet, so unfortunately for her, she left a sticky and stinky mess to be cleaned up in her bathroom.

"Ugh--that's gross, Lexi, I'm out of here. You're such a girly girl, can't hold down your food and beer. I'm going back to bed. Call me if you need me, otherwise, I'm going back to sleep." Karen ran out of the bathroom into the bedroom under the safety of the covers. She held on tight to the silky cotton fabric of her pillow as she wished herself to sleep. Karen's wish for sleep didn't seem to come true with all the commotion that Alexis carried on in the bathroom with the mop bucket.

Alexis silently sang to herself as she mopped away the filth and stench of her internal self. She thought about both the rocky twist and turns of her and Karen's relationship, and the seemingly disappointing moments that she often faced with her overly religious mother.

I wish the world could see me through my eyes, see me as the woman who I have always wanted to be. See me as a free spirit, one that would fly to the highest hill just to express the true nature of my identity. And then, I'll touch the rainbow as if it was a cool stratosphere of hope for my generation and me. I wish that I was straight, but I love being gay. Alexis announced to herself, as she finally had come to her senses that she mopped over the same spot at least seven times.

She put away the mop and the mop bucket, and then headed back into the bedroom where she found a partially naked Karen in her undergarments fast asleep under the covers. Karen's wish for sleep had come true, but her wish would be awakened by a slightly aroused twenty-two year old Alexis Carter.

Flowers

"**W**elcome to our home, Pastor Saunders, it's sad to hear that Sista Rita has gone on to be with the Lord," Brenda said with a grin. *That ole' heffa, girlfriend had it coming. I knew the first day they put her in charge of the missionary board that her pressure would go up. The woman was just too prideful. An abomination if you ask me.*

"Well, Brenda, we just try to do our best with what we have. We know that this life is barely a breath, and then boom we are gone. Although our physical deaths are led into our spiritual eternity, we still must die to the flesh daily." His eyes were glued on Brenda while chasing after the shadow that kept appearing and disappearing in the hallway, he could not grasp who or what it was. "Is there anyone else here right now, Brenda?" He asked with an irritated tone.

"Yes, Pastor Saunders, my daughter, Alexis, is in the back room sleeping. Supposedly, she was a little hung over when she arrived here this morning. She knew that you were coming. She should be up by now." She looked down at her watch; the time was two in the afternoon.

The pastor snickered a bit at Brenda's willingness to not hold back her tongue, even if it meant hurting her own children in the process.

"For the millionth time, Brenda, please call me, Malcolm. Enough with the formalities, we are family now." He loosened his tie, he thought about his wife Urethra and his two sons' that were waiting for him in their SUV."

Brenda gave him a quick glance as she reminisced once more on the love they shared in their early twenties. She even took to thinking about how the news of Pastor Malcolm Saunders having a love child would fare in the church.

Brenda, her daughters and grandchildren had frequented Square Pentecostal Church on the regular. On one particular Sunday in church, Pastor Saunders had spoken about 'letting loose the secrets.' He said, "Secrets will tarry our lives to the grave, and there won't be enough flowers left to cover the filth and stench of generational secrets."

Brenda and the kids were sitting on the very front row that particular Sunday, dressed to impress. With the help of a few of their fellow saints, Brenda and her children began to receive more help than that which came from the government. While the members of the church pitched in, she was able to purchase some of the finest linens for her children, and Brandy couldn't have been happier, she knew that she was going to church looking and feeling her best.

As Pastor Saunders continued to preach his *conviction* service, members of the church were unusually quiet; some even shared awkward stares and snares, they hoped that no one would have ever noticed the guilt that resonated from within their spirit. Brenda was a mess on her own; she just could not keep still in her seat. *Only if Pastor knew that this daughter of mine is his, or maybe I should just keep that a secret.* Brenda thought. She definitely favors him, she has to be his daughter.

Urethra noticed Brenda's restlessness out of the corner of her eyes; she had become acquainted to Brenda's outburst and sudden spasms of the 'Holy Spirit' til' she didn't think much of those particular episodes anymore. Brenda was devising a plan in her heart to tell Pastor Saunders everything. She wanted to release all she had to him. She wanted to not only remind him of the good times they had together, but also tell him how much she missed him, and that he and Michael Lewis were the only men that she had loved in her lifetime.

As Pastor Saunders kept preaching and purged the hearts of the men and women of the church, Brenda could not keep silent anymore, she stood up, and then the roar of whispers filled the sanctuary.

Brenda looked to the left to see the disdain in her daughter Sabrina's eyes, and then she looked over to the right and noticed the shame that exuded from Alexis.

"Pastor, I---uh---I---believe that this here is your daughter." She pointed in Alexis's direction. Immediately, the whispers were no longer, with the oohs---ahhs--- and gasp, the church sounded like Monday morning rush hour traffic, and Brenda had just blew the horn that started it all.

Urethra was appalled, and Pastor Saunders was tight lipped. Once again, Brenda put a whole service on hold, and the gawking session had begun. Pastor Saunders regained his composure under the guise of an angry Urethra, "Um---um-- sister Brenda. What are you implying? I have two precious children that are seated next to my lovely wife there." He tried to brush it off, he hoped to maybe even score a few points with his wife, but her face was redder than a white woman having a heart attack. Her fist was cuffed and she was ready to fight.

Somebody gone see Jesus for-real this great morning, and it ain't gone be me. This heffa got a lot of nerve to be in my church this whole time, screwing with my husband. Somebody better tell me something, or some hell will be raised up in this church. Oh, I'll take my Jesus suit off in a quick New York minute. Urethra contemplated, she reflected back on her days in the projects.

After much pulling and tension from her daughters, Brenda spoke once more.

"After doing the math, Pastor Saunders, and looking at this here girl besides me, then looking at you. Yawl two is some kin, you are Alexis' father." She said with confidence, and then took her seat while she idly rocked back and forth in her pew.

Urethra just about fell out from the news, Pastor Saunders placed the microphone down, then hurried from the pulpit to deliver the moderately chilled with crushed ice spring water to his wife, which was held in a twelve ounce glass. When he arrived to her seat, he coached Urethra to take solid, slow breaths, and then he introduced her to the glass of water. "Breathe, sweetie, breathe," Pastor Saunders said, as he took a quick glance at Brenda, he gave her a look that was uncharacteristic of his position, it was the evil eye. The deacons of the church also rushed to the front of the church, two went to assist Urethra and the Pastor, while the other was adamant about escorting Brenda and her kids out of the church.

The Pastor raised his hands and said, "No, leave them here deacon, if this here is my child from a relationship years ago, I would like to know more about it. In fact, I need to know some facts, and there is bound to be a DNA test. She's not the only woman to come up to me and make a bold statement like that, and nor would she be the last. I made many bad choices in my youth, deacon, but after taking a DNA test with the other women who claimed I was their baby's daddy, they all came up wrong."

Pastor Saunders shook his head as he continued to tend to his wife; he silently spoke 1 Peter 5:10 to himself as he thought about all the confusion that ensued in the church.

"People think that because I have pastor as a title to my name. That I have all of a sudden come up to some grand amounts of money. I've had all kind of women come out of the blue, women I never even met before in my life, claiming that I'm the father of their child. If people only knew how much this position puts a strain on my family, especially my wife, they wouldn't be so eager to accept this call. But you see, deacon, I was more than called, I was chosen by God to do His will, and that fact I cannot deny."

The deacon still held on to Brenda as if he was about to cuff her and throw her in the back of a squad car, never to return to Square Pentecostal Church.

"Deacon, let go of her, I know her beyond the four walls of the church." The deacon let go of the grip he had on a frustrated Brenda, and backed away just as she was ten seconds from releasing her pepper spray on him.

"She and I had a history together a long time ago, and I did my best to pretend that she was just some crazy woman coming in here screaming my name. I knew her from the first day she walked in this church. I never forget a woman's voice."

Urethra listened to her husband's confession, she was hurt by the secret that he harbored, and she was crushed, she felt embarrassed that he said it all in the front pew where she resided.

Pastor Saunders released everything and was only just an inch away from his wife, so he made sure that he brushed up his confession a bit, "I did not know that she had a child by me, at least as so she claims. Like I said, I am willing to do a DNA test to prove either way if that beautiful girl over there is mine." He pointed at a somber Alexis, seemingly stuck in the middle of the whole circus that came to the church. "Then, I will do the best I can to be the father that I need to be to her as well. I will love her like I love my two boys that God and my beautiful wife gave to me. Otherwise, as of right now everything else is just here say."

He reached out his hands towards his wife to give her a hug, but she backed up in her seat, she was hurt by the news, and wanted nothing to do with him or the church at that particular moment.

One of the other deacons of the church went to the podium, he called everyone to order, then gave the benediction. "Church is dismissed," the deacon said.

The pastor and his family had already left out the church while the deacon gave the benediction. Brenda and her family were left to exit the church with stares and snarls from their fellow church members. It surely was a day to remember for everyone who attended that particular Sunday service at Square Pentecostal Church.

*****

"Brenda, are you okay?" Pastor Saunders looked dumbfounded, never before had Brenda been so quiet in his presence.

She released herself from her thoughts. "Yeah, Pastor Saunders. I mean, Malcolm, I just was thinking about that time five years ago when I stood up in the church to tell you that Alexis was your daughter."

"Yeah Brenda, you almost broke up a happy home from that incident. My wife thought I was cheating on her. You know how Urethra can be. You go to the church. I was her first and she knew no other man, she's very protective of me, and you know how much I love that woman." He grinned, happy to know that. That particular issue was far behind them, although issues of jealousy often times creped its head on him and Urethra's conversations.

"So, what brings you here today, Pastor?" She quickly covered her mouth with her right hand, punished herself for the formalities.

Before he could even clear his throat, he had to remember what he was there for. *Oh, that's right.* He finally remembered that he was there to talk about Alexis's child, Kita. Once he found out five years prior that Alexis indeed was his child, he volunteered to do everything in his power to at least try to make up for lost time and help the Carter family the best way he knew how. During that same year of the revelations at the church and the positive DNA results, Brenda revealed to Pastor Saunders that she was on the verge of giving Kita up for adoption, and that a family had already inquired about Kita, who was turning two at the time.

Kita was such a beautiful child, and the older she got the more she took on her father's traits, while she shared her mother's deep dimples and straight black hair. Pastor Saunders was less than enthusiastic about the news of giving Kita up for adoption, therefore he knew that he had to do everything in his power to make it right, he couldn't fathom the thought of his grandchild living in a home full of strangers. So—he did the unthinkable, he begged and pleaded with his wife to get custody of Kita. It was already a stressful situation for Urethra and she wasn't having any part of the Carters at that time.

The sudden news of Alexis being his child was already enough to make her roll over with fury, but the thought of an adoption was way out of the question.

Kita's fate was on the line and there seemed to be no budging out of Urethra, until—she received counsel from one of her best friends.

"Listen, girl, I know that Malcolm done let you down and all, but you have to look at it from his perspective as well. The man probably didn't want to tell you about that Brenda chick in fear of you overreacting. So—look at that, you have overreacted as usual, not saying that he was right. I'm just saying to look at it from his perspective."

"I know, girl, I really do love Malcolm, and you know how my man has been good to me, I'm just afraid of losing him to some trifling project chick. You know I'm from the streets, so I know how women in general can get in a man's front pocket, more or less a woman from the hood that is really up on her game."

"Listen, Urethra, I've seen cheating men, I know them like a bad case of the measles, your husband does not seem like the guy who goes out and cheat. I'm not saying that because he's a pastor and all, I'm just saying from my interactions with him, he just doesn't seem like a man who rolls that way. Of course, I'm not saying that I can tell them all, but he just seems like he is really trying to do right by you and the kids."

"I know, I know." Urethra smiled as she thought about how Pastor Saunders was the perfect husband and father in so many ways.

"That's why he wants to keep this grandbaby of his; he wants to make up for lost time. Men like the sense of accomplishment, and a good man will do anything in his power to protect his kids and his kids, kids too. What's one more mouth to feed, you told me that she's a pretty girl, and your sons will have them a little sister to play with."

"I always wanted a daughter," Urethra confessed, as she internalized the idealism of having Kita around the house.

"Girl, just think about it, and call me once you made up your mind," her friend had hung up the phone and left Urethra with a Bounty tissue roll of information to think about.

And just from that conversation and much prayer, Urethra agreed to adopt Kita. Kita had been living with Pastor Saunders and Urethra for five years, and she had grown to be a very intelligent and inquisitive seven year old in grade school. It was at the age of four when Pastor Saunders and Urethra attempted to explain to her all that happened and why she was put up for adoption. Although she had the opportunity to see her mother all the time, they knew that she found it strange that she was living with them instead of with her mother and grandmother like Sabrina's children.

Pastor Saunders snapped from his memory bank. "What brought me here today is the fact that

Kita is telling us that she wants to live back with you all. She wants to be closer to her mother." He paused, the subject of Kita was always a hard reminder for Brenda and him, when they found out that Alexis indulged in lesbian activities with her best friend Sylvia.

"Well, you know why I put the girl up for adoption, and I am very grateful that you and Urethra decided to take her in." She couldn't hold it any longer; a tear sprang down from her cheek to her t-shirt.

"It's okay, Brenda, I felt that it was the least that I could do considering the fact that I wasn't there for our daughter, Alexis. Well, quite frankly, I did not know that I had any children outside those that were born of Urethra." He shook his head in silence; he wished that he could have done things a lot different in the days of his youth.

"Listen, I understand, I thought she was Michael's baby. You and I were just, well, you know."

He finished where she left off. "It's okay to say it, we were very close, let's not go into details, but the blood test proved that I am the father. So-- everything happens for a reason, God is not in the business of making mistakes. But like I said, Kita wants to be here with her mother, I know that you forced Alexis to give up all of her parental rights, but I think that this may just be the better fit for her. We've had Kita for five years; she's doing well in school. As a matter of fact, we need to pick her up in fifteen minutes." He shook his head at his watch. *Where does the time go, Lord, where does the time go?*

The shadow that had disappeared from the hallway minutes prior had returned, upon the return Pastor Saunders was able to make out the shadow with detail, "I want my daughter back now!" Alexis said, half-drunk, with a fierce attitude.

"That's just what we were discussing, but I've been to your apartment." A loud horn rang through the neighborhood. "That has to be my wife. Look here, Alexis, you have a one-bedroom apartment, if your daughter stays anywhere, it would have to be here. Why don't you get rid of your apartment and move back in with your mom and sisters for a little while, I'm sure they won't mind. Then, you and Kita can spend all the time you want together without worrying about my wife and I's schedule." He referenced the beautiful home in Kendall; he put Brenda in a house there just twenty minutes south of the projects, Brenda and the girls loved the new house.

Of course Urethra was less than thrilled, but because of the fact that the church was paying the mortgage on their home and Pastor Saunders had received a twenty-percent raise on his day job as a civil engineer, she was reluctant to allow him to pay the mortgage on the Carter home. With four bedrooms and two baths, everyone was comfortable and safer in Brenda's new home. Alexis had left and gone off to college for a short stint, all to have returned and signed a lease on her own apartment.

She and her mother could never get along, so she found that living in her own place was the best option for her.

Alexis's apartment was in the heart of Opa-locka, Florida, right off of northwest 132nd Street. She intended on moving back to Tallahassee for school, but work was good in Miami, all her hopes and dreams on finishing her college education had vanished, but the one thing that could bring joy to her life for good, was the one person they managed to keep her away from, *her daughter.*

"So—what did my mother say about me moving here with Kita?" *Although I would never live back here, she made my life a living hell the moment she found out about Sylvia and I.*

"I actually haven't gotten around to talking to her about that. I was hoping to kind of feel you out before I presented that to her." He smiled as he gazed on into the eyes of his prodigal daughter. He was so afraid for the life that she chose with the heavy drinking, partying, and choice in woman. But he knew that the last thing he wanted to do was keep her away from her child.

"You know what, ya'll ain't right." Alexis stomped down the hallway and slammed the room door. She saddled herself on top of the bed and cried and cried herself to sleep. Her moaning had been heard through the hallway, all the way to the kitchen where Pastor Saunders and Brenda were sharing their goodbyes.

"Malcolm, I'm sorry you had to witness that. That girl is a little unstable right now. Now, do you see why I don't want her keeping Kita? She'll probably want to take my grandbaby back up there to Tallahassee with her." Brenda showed no remorse, she kept still in her chair with a straight face.

Pastor Saunders was moved, his heart was heavy. "Brenda. That was the sounds of a woman who craves the presence of her child. Those cries were cries of love; I don't believe that she would hurt her child. Listen, I'm not trying to get rid of Kita, Urethra and I have loved her like she's our own. The boys even like the fact that they have a younger sister that they can tease, they sure are very protective of her as well." He heard the sound of the horn blazing once more. That time it was even louder, the neighborhood dogs were so aggravated by it that their barks could be heard a few blocks down the street as well.

Pastor Saunders rose from his chair. "Goodbye, Brenda, we'll talk about this some more another day. We have to pick up Kita."

"Okay, Malcolm," Brenda said politely, as she met him to the door. "Take care, I'll see you soon." As soon as she closed the door upon his exit, she watched him through the window as he opened the door to his black SUV. With the vehicle no longer in sight, she broke down. She cried silent tears, she wanted nothing but the best for her daughter and her grandchild, but she just could not muster the lifestyle that Alexis had chosen.

Lord God, help this family. You have given us much with this beautiful house and I thank you for a stable teaching job with the County. But Lord, we need your direction. Help me Lord not to look at Pastor Saunders no other way than that of righteousness and holiness. Help my daughter Lord God, help my daughter to turn straight, take her from the narrow pits of destruction Lord, and seed her into the right spirit. Make her whole again Lord Jesus; renew in her the right spirit. A bold spirit that seeks after you, this I pray in Jesus name, amen.

Just as Brenda finished praying, a strange sound came from the door. It just about startled Brenda into a cardiac arrest, she yelled out, "Who is it?"

"Yes, ma'am," the stranger yelled to the top of his lungs, "I'm from UPS and I have a package that is here for a Brenda Carter." He paused for a moment, and waited for a response, he had already been to the door ten seconds more than he anticipated, and he grew impatient.

Brenda responded, "Well, I don't know anything about receiving a package."

"It's addressed to a Brenda Carter, is that you, ma'am?" He tapped his feet on the porch; he was ready to just leave the box without a signature since a signature was not required for that particular shipment.

"Yes. That's me." She drew closer to the door, she confirmed through the peephole that it was in fact a man from UPS as she also dually noticed the big brown truck parked to the side of the road, she was comfortable enough to open the door as she received the package.

"Thank you, Ma'am, you have a nice day." He leaped from the porch and sped off to his next destination. Meanwhile, Brenda carefully observed the package, she noticed how horizontally long the package was, yet vertically thin. *This is not what I think it is. And who in the world is this from.*

Brenda took to opening the package at the kitchen table; it was a box full of red roses, twelve roses to be exact. There was a note attached on one of the stems of the flowers. It read…*Hey, baby. I've been missing you. I sent you these flowers because I'll be out of the pen in twelve days; they are letting me out early for good behavior. I hope that you and my daughters are doing well. I can't wait to see you so that we can finally be the family that we were intended to be. Love always, your boo, Michael.*

Brenda almost fell back in her chair upon reading the note, she never told Michael that Pastor Saunders was Alexis's true father, nor did she share with him her new address. She was both stunned and afraid at the same time, the last person she needed in her new life was Michael Lewis.

Desires

O h, how I crave the soft, warm and tender touch of a woman right next to me. She doesn't have to be built, just good enough for me to explore into the deepest core of my fantasies. She can caress me with her thoughtless dreams and pull me to the side with her selfish ambitions. She will get hers and I will get mines.

Oh, how I love the blessings of the sweet lips of a female, she'll hold me in her grasp as if I was made of sugar and cinnamon. Our hearts will collapse into our empty space, and then I'll erase all memories, which will deface her and I being together. Yes, this is what I want, I want it now, and no longer can I wait for Karen to come around. This is my desire. This is how I feel. How could this type of affection be so wrong when it feels so real?

"Alexis Carter, snap out of it. This is the third day in a row that you have been daydreaming in this office. Are you okay?" The man inquired.

Alexis pulled herself together, she had a few more hours on the clock, but it felt like an eternity, her hormones were screaming. "Yeah, I'm good, just been having some family trouble lately. That's all." She waited til' the man left her cubicle and exhaled a sigh of relief.

She worked for a telemarketing company in South Miami-Dade, her job was just twenty minutes south of her mother's home in Kendall, and thirty-five to forty minutes south of her apartment in Opa-locka.

That manager is so nosey, it's my fault, shouldn't have been daydreaming.

She made fourteen dollars an hour receiving customer service calls on behalf of big brand companies, recently she'd been putting some of her money aside to save up for Tallahassee, with a major such as political science, Tallahassee was the perfect place to be for politics.

"Hello, this is Alexis Carter with Studs Electronics, how may I help you?" She twirled her fingers a bit, even sketched a stick figure on her notepad as she waited for the person to respond on the other line. She figured that they must have hung up, she looked at the phone line again and noticed that they were still on. With each call being monitored by her boss and boss's boss for accuracy and customer retention, she said, "Hello," once more in the hopes that the person on the line would actually say something.

Their customer service line had been known to be plagued by prank callers trying to win free stuff, or just downright have an agenda to be disrespectful for fun's sake. Then, there were the mystery shoppers who called in for quality control on behalf of the companies, which farmed out their work to Sunshine Telemarketing Agency.

With no response and in no means prepared to be *punked*, Alexis moved her mouse over to press the hang-up feature on her computer screen. Just as soon as her mouse hovered over the hang-up button, a familiar voice expressed their greetings. Although familiar, she still wasn't quite sure who it was.

"This is Studs Electronics, how may I help you?" She tried to decipher both the person and the point of the call as she noticed her time meter was approaching red, a signal, which alerted the manager of her time on the phone. All calls that ended up in the red received the manager's immediate attention and would at often times be listened to at the time of the call.

"Well, it seems that this was the only way to get in contact with you?" The man said on the other line.

Well aware of her manager's *red* procedures she grew impatient with the man.

"Well, do I know you from somewhere, sir? How may I assist you with your electronics?" She still wasn't sure who the man was, but she was sure ready to get off the phone, she also knew that she had to keep the conversation quick and as professional as possible, with the thought of her boss listening on the other end. Her job was at stake.

The man paused and said, "Alexis, you know who I am. I have been calling you for the last few days." And from that confession immediately she knew who it was, she wanted to scream.

"Listen, Michael, I am at work, and I don't have time for this right now. I'm happy that you called, but you and ma need to talk. Apparently--" She caught herself, she didn't want to give any hint at the revelations of Pastor Saunders being her real father.

She thought to herself for a second, then looked at the time and knew that she had to wrap up their over the phone meet and greet very quickly.

"I'm sorry, Michael; I have no desires to talk to you right now. Besides, I'm at work, and I could lose my job because now this is considered a personal call. Unless you need some help with your electronic equipment purchased through Studs Electronics, I will have to let you go." She said curtly.

"Okay. That's cool." He looked at the prison cells, freedom was close at hand. "Well, I get out in three days; I'll see you and your mom real soon." He waited for a reply.

"Okay. That's good to hear, have to go now, bye." She released the phone and was happy to press the hang-up button. To her surprise, her manager did not rush over to her desk for going into the red like he normally would.

*****

"Hey, I've been waiting all day for you." The young lady in the pink skirt and matching pink top said at the door step of Alexis's apartment.

Surprised by the visitor, Alexis did not know what to expect. Perhaps the dogma of memories past had come back to haunt her, as the passions which once eroded their friendship had returned with a vengeance.

The young lady counted with her fingers and signaled for a response from the very surprised

Alexis. "Well, now aren't you going to say something?" The girl took to looking deep in the eyes of Alexis, she noticed that her passion still lingered and longed for her very existence. This very revelation gave her pause to at least applaud herself internally.

Given the courage to speak and restless at her front door Alexis said, "Sylvia, what in the world are you doing here? I thought you were in college in Chicago somewhere. I don't know, I mean, what's going on with you?" She released the key from her right hand and unlocked the door with one twist. She motioned for Sylvia to come inside as the two sat on her brown leather couch, the second destination for which many dirty deeds had been committed. Of course, the first destination of choice had been her bedroom mattress, but on nights when she was extremely drunk, she cared less where she and her female lovers played around, even the floor has had its share of sin.

"Yeah, I am in college in Chicago at Roosevelt University; I have one more year left in my Creative Writing program, I plan to be a bestselling author one day."

"For real girl...Are you serious?" The excitement showed all throughout Alexis's radiantly beautiful skin, she let her hair back and it revealed the lusciousness of her natural beauty, she was the model type.

Sylvia being the recipient of that excitement thought she'd add a little spice to the conversation.

It's been five years since the two had seen or spoken to each other, they had a lot of catching up to do. After being banned from each other's lives after that one evening of intimacy and pleasure, neither family knew exactly how to embrace the matters of them being different.

"Yeah, girl, Roosevelt University is one of the best when it comes down to creative writing." She smiled. A little tickled at the thought of seeing her name at the top of the New York Times Bestseller's list, she would even be pleased if she made Essence and USA Today's bestseller's list as well.

"So you gone be like the Toni Morrison, Maya Angelou type?" She leaned her head back, thrilled for her best friend. At least if she could still use the term *best friend* since it's been so long since the two had seen each other.

"Yeah, girl, of course, I got mad respect for them, but you also got to check out writers like Earnest Hemmingway, James Joyce, and George Orwell. Oh, you also have to check out my man Richard Wright, he wrote that book called *Black Boy*, I read that book last semester, it had me in tears." She said with utter excitement, she felt more and more comfortable with the thought of being in the presence of Alexis.

"Word," Alexis inquired.

"Yeah," Sylvia said, "You also have to check out some of the other author's that be on their grind but don't get much mainstream credit. I was doing a Google search on like black writers, and of course, you'd be surprised how many black authors are doing their thing today. I did the search for my project I had last semester." She caught her breath.

"Girl, you know I hardly read, I mean besides a little Zane from here and there and maybe a little E. Lynn Harris, there aren't many books out there on my issues and my perspective as being a lesbian." She put her head down; she knew that it was sort of a sour subject for the both.

"Well, just to let you know, I'm clean." Sylvia said with cheer, it forced Alexis to immediately pick her head up and decode what Sylvia was referring to.

"What do you mean by you're clean, I never took you for an attic." She looked at her friend suspiciously, she thought about all that happened over the course of five years. She never would have imagined that her best friend was a crack addict or habitual alcoholic; at least the alcoholic title belonged to her.

Sylvia recognized that Alexis was confused by her statement, she decided to break it down. "No, silly, I don't do drugs, well, maybe weed every now and then. But surely, I have never sniffed or shot up coke.

"So what are you talking about then?" Alexis was still confused.

"I'm talking about being clean from that lifestyle of lesbianism; I'm talking about being free. I have a boyfriend up there in Chicago now and we are making plans on getting married and everything. He said that he wants to wait to propose to me sometime next year, right around the time I graduate."

Alexis was disheartened, she couldn't believe her ears, the very woman who got her into so much trouble, although the two shared in the blame, but she could not imagine the woman who she shared passionate desires with, was walking as a free woman. In simpler terms, she could not believe Sylvia's confession of being *straight*.

"Alexis, are you okay? You act as if you have just seen a ghost." She understood that there would be confusion in her confession.

"Honestly." She shook her head. "I just can't believe that you out of all people done went straight, you know what I'm saying. I mean, you always had boyfriends, so that part doesn't really mean much to me. So how do you like really know that you are straight and not just some fad that you decided was the next best thing because society says so?"

"I know because I met God on a deeper level, and I met this professor guy on this college tour. The Professor's name is Paul Stringer, girl he's so handsome. Anyway he himself struggled with homosexuality and he was just at our university to give his testimony and introduce the authors of the upcoming book, *Out of Order*. They gave each student a copy of their pre-published manuscript for review. Of course, I don't remember the name of the two brothers that were a part of that book, but the manuscript was good, it changed my life."

"Oh, really," she questioned once more, still wasn't sold on Sylvia being straight.

"Yeah, I mean of course, it all didn't happen at one time, it took a lot of discipline, praying and having a true desire to wanting to change. You feel me?" She pleaded; she hoped that something would make sense to her longtime friend and partner.

Alexis wanted to change the subject so she decided to switch lanes. "So you never told me why you came here at my door steps today when obviously you should be in Chicago, and how in the world did you get my address?"

"Well, I came down here for my Grandmother Rita's funeral, it was like a few days ago, I thought you were going to be there. But since I noticed you weren't there, I saw your sister, Brandy, there and she gave me your address. Of course, your mother mean mugged me, I thought for certain that she'd alert you that I was in town, or at least your sister should have told you."

"No telling how bad my mother done brain washed my sisters about me, I'm sorry to hear about your grandmother, I believe that I was working that day."

"Any plans on going back up to school?" Sylvia asked with a long face, she knew that her freedom from lesbianism came at a cost, a high cost of dying to the flesh daily. In the presence of Alexis, her flesh could remember the steamy events that they shared together, even the smell of Alexis's perfume was enough to mildly arouse Sylvia's hidden parts, and she could not believe how strong the struggle was at that particular moment.

Alexis noticed the sudden awkwardness in Sylvia's composure, she held off Sylvia's question to ask, "Are you okay?" She smirked. *Maybe the truth about Sylvia being clean will come out after all, I could use a little under the sheets action anyway. Lord knows the very essence of her presence is about to make me explode.*

"Yeah, I'm good; I just need to get out of here. I don't feel so good all of a sudden. It's kind of warm in here as well. Can you turn on the AC or something?" She inquired, as she looked at her purse, her keys were dead center ready for her to take off and head back to her mother's house because she had been delivered for three years, she felt that she could withstand the temptation, even if it meant that the struggle would intensify.

Alexis got up with pleasure to place the air-conditioner on a cooler temperature; she had a wide smile on her face for which Sylvia could not see. *At least she still has the hots for me, wouldn't want to ruin the engagement,* she devilishly thought to herself.

While she returned to her seat, she noticed that Sylvia was missing; she knew that she didn't hear the door open, so she couldn't have left her apartment. Her one bedroom apartment was only but so big, and then she heard it, the sounds of the roaring of the toilet, Sylvia had slipped into the bathroom without her knowing. What Sylvia was actually doing in the restroom was of another matter.

Sylvia did not use the restroom for the functions of releasing bodily fluids; she went in there to pray for God to continue to release the spiritual demons that were warring against her soul. The cravings for relations with Alexis grew heavier, and she knew that if she did not hit the front door of the apartment quick, there would have been some consequences.

Alexis sensed that there was something wrong by Sylvia's continuous presence in the restroom after the first flush. So she decided to test Sylvia's spirit and confession, she pulled off her work t-shirt and loosened her bra, she displayed only that of the firmness in her breast, the mirror of her youth and tenacity of her vigor. She desired to be with Sylvia, even if it meant to make her friend fall.

Sylvia exited the bathroom and into the living room, she did not believe her eyes, but she was better prepared for what she knew was to come. She was saddened and yet sympathetic with Alexis's topless display, nevertheless the center of Sylvia's breast protruded a tenth of an inch, at least they too served as an acknowledgement and reminder of her past desires. She walked on over to Alexis, and with a panicked craze, Alexis moaned, she was ready to be touched again by her female friend. She was ready to light back the candle of their affection, and ready to break the bed down.

Sylvia on the other hand had a different plan in mind. *God help me in the name of Jesus I pray that you release me of this unnatural thing. Help me and my friend here who has fallen victim to a lie.* With Alexis's eyes still closed and only able to absorb the breathing of her friend, Sylvia picked up Alexis work t-shirt from off the leather couch and placed it neatly back onto Alexis's sexually appealing frame.

Alexis immediately opened her eyes, a little dumbfounded at first, as she noticed Sylvia pick her keys out from the center of her purse and head on out the door. Not another word was said between the two as Sylvia revved the engine of her 2013 BMW M3. The BMW M3 was a birthday gift from her dad for good grades in school.

Although the two did not share in final goodbyes, their body language said everything their mouths could not. Alexis was disgusted and ashamed of her actions, while Sylvia felt the bruising of a near failing situation.

Wow, that was close, now I understand the dynamics to the term 'dying to the flesh daily' and the consequences of going back into a lifestyle of lesbianism, but never did I think that the urges for another woman could present itself to be so strong after three years of being delivered.

Like a crack head to a broken beat, or perhaps a broken record, so is the cycle of sin if it is not dealt with in its proper place. Jesus was tempted by the devil on a number of occasions, and He won. He beat the odds with the greatest tempter, but man in his or her decaying flesh is often tripped over and succumbs to the beatings of the devil. Sylvia fought hard and was released, but the remnants of a desire for which she thought was lost and forgotten, had now brought her to question her very essence of deliverance.

I feel so dirty; I hate feeling rejected like that. It's almost as if I can just scrub my body with a Brillo pad topped off with a double-headed razor. Even then, if Alexis were to take those extreme measures, it could not wash away the filth she felt inside, nothing but the blood of Jesus.

Seasons Change

"**W**ho can make me whole again?
Nothing but the blood of Jesus."
Brenda sang her tunes in the shower;
it was an unspoken family tradition for everyone to
sing in the shower, at least a tradition for which
Brenda made up. She said that it was freeing to sing
in the shower, no one there to judge or laugh at you,
just an opportunity for you to be one with the shower
and God. "No other name I know. That makes me
white as snow." She continued with her song. Since
converting to Christianity, she switched her songs
from many of the bump and grind tunes of Rhythm
and Blues, to the soul stirring music of Gospel. She
loved the conversion; her spirit often felt at peace.

Boom-Boom-Boom, a loud knock was at her
bathroom door, Brenda almost slipped in the tub at the
sound, it was Sabrina warning her that dinner was
ready, and Alexis and Pastor Saunders called to let her
know that they were on their way. Of course, Brenda
was agitated by the certain surprise and disturbance of
peace, she said, "Are you sure the turkey is ready?"

"Yes, Ma, I know how to cook, I have two
growing boys you know." Sabrina said with a slight
tude.

Satisfied with her eldest daughter's answer, she
went back to singing her tunes and prepared herself
for her final rinse. *These girls will kill me before I hit fifty.*
Brenda thought to herself as she began to dry her

round black bottom and the few specs of water that was hugging her chest.

Meanwhile, Sabrina was in the kitchen putting the finishing touches on the perfectly tender, lightly blackened, and stuffing rich turkey. It was that time of year where families gathered and pretended to like one another. But then again with family, no one had to like the other, as long as love flowed strong, family would always find a way to get along. Sabrina's two boys were giggling and having a good time at the kitchen table, til' the doorbell rang them out of their unofficial playtime with one another.

Sabrina caught her breath as the second sounds of the doorbell nearly made her drop the collard greens all over the kitchen floor. "I'm coming, I'm coming." She yelled out, angry and agitated at the same time. By then her two boys had already ran to the door, but they knew better to open it to strangers.

Meanwhile, Brenda had just finished putting on her best red dress, and she sprayed a descent amount of perfume to supposedly set the mood.

"Mommy, it's Lexi at the door." Sabrina's eldest son yelled to the top of his lungs. This was his way to get permission to open the door without being reprimanded.

"Go ahead and let her in boy," she said while stirring the greens, and she added her little spices to what Brenda had already seasoned.

"Girl, just what are you doing?" Brenda caught Sabrina off guard; Sabrina hadn't noticed her presence and obviously didn't get a whiff of her heavy smelling perfume.

"Mama, I was just you know." she stopped talking; she knew that Brenda wasn't listening to a word she was saying.

Alexis had entered the kitchen with her nephews lingering on both sides of her.

"Well, I'm glad that you can make it," Sabrina looked over at Alexis suspiciously. *I hope the girl ain't high or nothing, she looks a royal mess.*

"Yeah, I'm good, the boss man let me off earlier than I expected. You know how that goes." She sighed, there was surely something that troubled her, but she couldn't really grasp what it was. *I'm sick.* She thought to herself as she took a seat in the kitchen while her nephews went back to doing what little seven and eight-year-old boys did, play around and act a fool.

"Well, praise God that you are employed, your sister here wouldn't get a job to save her soul." Brenda chuckled a bit. She knew that Sabrina would react, so she just waited out the five seconds she knew it would take for Sabrina to absorb everything she had said.

And her reaction. "That's because I got's me a good baby daddy that supports me. I get three checks a month, so, why work? Don't act like you don't know what I'm talking about, mama, I know about all them checks you used to get for us. Just because that Ricky Wilder cat ain't ever step up to the plate and handle his business beyond being a sperm donor, don't mean ya'll got to hate on me." She smiled, and then opened the oven to check on the yellowy crusty edges of the corn bread.

Alexis was in shock, she was in her own zone, she didn't say anything, but then she was called out as being a hater by her own sister. "Now how come you two done got me in this mess, I didn't say anything, but you done pulled Ricky Wilder into the mix. That boy is history; we already know that he's a dirt bag, no need of rubbing it even further in the ground." She said her piece and zoned out again, Brenda was elated. She set it all up from the start, happy to see a little fussing again. Ever since they moved to their new home in Kendall, arguments had been few and far between, partly because Alexis had already moved to her own place.

There was another chime of the doorbell. That time it seemed to be even louder than the first; everyone including the boys had become unnaturally quiet in the kitchen due to the shock of the doorbell penetrating their eardrums. The only thing left to bake were the sweet potato pies, which Brenda slaved over the night before all the way into the wee hours of the morning. She carefully crafted the sugar, evaporated milk, vanilla, eggs and cinnamon into the Refrigerated Pie Crust. She made approximately ten pies for which she sat them each in the refrigerator to absorb the rich textures of flavor for which they were blended with love to settle at the bottom of the crust.

Sabrina slowly pursued the door as she took a quick peek out the window. It was Pastor Saunders and his family, his two boys, Urethra and Kita; they were all huddled up at the door, ready for someone to welcome them in. They did not see Sabrina peeking at them through the window, Urethra grew impatient and rang the doorbell a third time.

"Just a minute," Sabrina said nicely, as she was only but two feet away from the door.

"Happy Thanksgiving!" Pastor Saunders and his family announced to Sabrina, as she was letting each one of them inside. They each sounded as if they had rehearsed their lines to a stage play; there wasn't one distinct sound in their greeting. Sabrina escorted them all to the kitchen as Kita and Alexis had immediately shared hugs and embraced one another.

"Mama, I love you, I'm so happy to see you." Kita said, as she just couldn't seem to let go of Alexis. Alexis was over the top in her emotions, immediately everyone felt the change in the atmosphere, with the showing of affection, it seemed as if there was a conversation brewing that they've been trying to avoid with each other for some time.

Brenda was disgusted by the sight of affection, she knew in her heart that Alexis would make at least a descent mother, but she just couldn't get over the lifestyle choice that Alexis had made to be with the same sex.

With the wit and wisdom that God had given Pastor Saunders, he knew that it was best to switch gears before the kitchen became even hotter than it was. He requested everyone to prepare to bow their heads and bless the food.

"But wait...Hold up, Pastor, where's my baby girl?" Brenda looked around; Brandy was nowhere to be seen.

Sabrina chimed in as she gathered her two boys closer to her, each one grabbed her hands as they prepared for the prayer. "Now you know that girl is a teenager, mama, you better watch that one. She spends more time in the bathroom now than ever before. She got them little boys' sexting her cell phone. I don't know, mama. She may not be the *angel* that you were wishing for." Sabrina said with pleasure, ever since she and Alexis had become pregnant, Brandy instantly became the *favorite child*. Of course, Sabrina and Alexis loved Brandy to death, they just hated the way she was treated with royalty, and they were treated like trash through the years just because they got themselves pregnant. Of course, they weren't asking to be rewarded for their pregnancies; but their sins had been forgotten by God. The blessing in their child bearing outweighed the capacity for which they bored their children. Their children were indeed a blessing from God.

"Brandy," Brenda yelled out, she chose to mute her eldest daughter. She knew deep inside that there was something up with Brandy as she sort of lived in a state of denial. Brandy was fifteen years old, a sophomore in high school at Miami Killian Senior High, she was the same age that Alexis was when she conceived her child, and Brenda was sore afraid that Brandy would fall in the footsteps of her sisters.

Of course, Brandy was attracted to boys just like most of the other girls that attended her school, but it was never anything that she was crazy about. With Brenda's constant shield of protection and weekly attendance at the church, Brandy was involved with so many extracurricular activities that she didn't have much time for anything else besides her studies, playing softball and her weekly choir rehearsals she attended on the weekend. But of course, in the sex-craved world of the media, no child, especially teenagers were totally immune to their surroundings. She often giggled to the talk of sex and enjoyed occasions of puppy love, but never did she take it farther than that. She wanted to be a kept woman like first lady Urethra. And she wanted to also be the one that broke the Carter curse of having children out of wedlock.

Lawd, if that girl is having sex, please tell me why? Why Lawd, why another daughter of mine can't keep up her panty lines? Give me the strength Lawd to talk to that girl. Lawd, she is so precious and I don't need another grandbaby now.

Brandy came running out from her room, happy as ever she greeted everyone with a wide smile.

"Well, what were you doing, Miss Popular?" Sabrina said swinging her head from left to right.

"You know what, now that Brandy is here, let's go ahead and bless the food." Pastor Saunders encouraged, he was the mediator in chief for the day.

"You got that right," Urethra agreed with her husband, she was agitated and tired of standing up holding hands. This was the first time her and her husband had Thanksgiving with the Carter's.

"Say the grace pastor, we're all ready, besides my pies have but five more minutes til' their done." Brenda said politely, yet slightly aggravated with Sabrina's apparent attack on her favorite child.

"Lord, we just thank you for the blessing of this food, Lord God. We thank you for the bonding of family to come together to be in a common place on a common day Lord God. Lord, we just pray that you bless the hands that have prepared this food for the nourishment of our body's, in Jesus name we pray. And all God's people say. Amen."

Everyone said amen, as Brenda rushed over to the oven to retrieve her pies, but she was caught in her tracks when she heard the blazing sound of the doorbell again. She looked around stupefied to see if anyone had invited another guest. Everyone gave her a resounding. "No." *Well, who could this be at my door this thanksgiving day?*

Brenda headed to the door, but not without calling Pastor Saunders over to follow behind her. As he and she were a few feet from the door, she looked out the window to see who it was, to her surprise she knew that the person that was standing out that door, would mean trouble for the inside. She immediately became flustered; she wasn't sure how to respond to the figure outside, as the individual rang the doorbell a second time.

Pastor Saunders was confused, they were right in front of the door, but Brenda refused to answer. He didn't get the same opportunity to glance out the window, and even if he did, he wouldn't have recognized the figure that was standing outside the door, just three inches of wood and metal was all that separated them. Pastor Saunders could not accept the silence from Brenda any longer as the bell rang a third time. He filled in where Brenda couldn't; he answered the door and said, "Well, who is it?" He was still behind Brenda, so he did not have the opportunity to peep through the tiny peephole.

"What do you mean, who is it? Is Brenda there?" the voice said.

Pastor Saunders immediately recognized that it could be trouble in paradise, he touched Brenda's garment to quietly get her attention. "Who is that man?"

Brenda finally regained her composure and quietly responded back. "It's Michael, Sabrina and Alexis' father. I mean, Sabrina's father, he doesn't know that he is not the father of Alexis. He sent me some flowers a couple of days ago saying that he was getting out of prison. I didn't think that he was serious though. And I surely did not invite him for Thanksgiving dinner." She shook her head; she was not prepared for that type of drama.

"So what do you want me to do? I can't lie to him. How did he even get your new address?" Pastor Saunders was very concerned for not only the safety and well-being of his immediate family, but also for Brenda's children as well.

"That's what I've been thinking about the last two few days. That scamp has ways of finding out information." Brenda sighed; she didn't know what to do. All she wanted was to have a happy and peaceful Thanksgiving, she was happy to smell the pies that were taken out by Sabrina in the kitchen; it reminded her of the real reason for Thanksgiving, and that was to cherish in the moment and be thankful for all that God had blessed her with.

"So, what do you want me to do, call the cops?" Pastor Saunders was not in the mood for drama, he just wanted to have a good time and go home in peace.

"Is she there cuz, I'm freezing?" Michael said through the door, aggravated that another man was answering the door for Brenda.

"No, you don't have to call the cops, he's harmless." Brenda whispered, she wished she could take back the *harmless* part of her statement.

"Yeah, she's here dude. How may I help you?" Pastor Saunders took offense.

"Tell her that Michael Lewis came by to see her."

"I'm right here, Michael, I've been here the whole time." Brenda couldn't contain herself. "What do you want from me, its Thanksgiving and I have family over. My food is getting cold and I did not invite you here." She said through the door, her levels of agitation went into third gear. She also was dreadfully hungry; she did her best to try to get rid of him.

"Listen, I'm just here to talk. That's all. And I wanted to see my girls, too, see how big they have gotten." He said with compassion, he was desperate for her to open the door; he pulled on every string he figured would work on her heart. But unbeknownst to him, Brenda wasn't buying what he was selling.

"Michael, why don't you just leave, you were not invited here. I don't know how you got my address, but I'm calling the cops if you don't leave."

Pastor Saunders had a look of shock from her statement of calling the cops. He suggested it, but she really said it.

"You gone call the pigs on me Brenda, after all we done been through together? Who is that man who answered the door anyway? I know he is still listening." Insecurity draped his subconscious mind like the blinds to a window, he was so blinded by his own fears and guilt, til' he only saw the situation from one point of view, *his*.

"Listen here, Michael; this man who is at this door is none of your concern. Now I have asked you nicely to leave my porch."

Alexis and Urethra heard the commotion at the front door escalating, so they dropped their forks in their plates and headed to the front door to find out who had been holding up Brenda and Pastor Saunders for over ten minutes.

"Ma, what's going on, who's outside the door?" Alexis said with a strange vigor, she was ready to fight if she had to.

"Hey, baby, is everything okay?" Urethra asked, as she analyzed her confused husband. Pastor Saunders had become a little distraught over all the commotion.

"Yeah, babe, I'm fine, just some man at the door bugging us. That's all." He responded with a light shrug of the shoulders and a mild headache, which didn't help the situation.

Michael Lewis had become infuriated when he heard the comment through the door that Pastor Saunders had spoken to Urethra. "I'm not just some man; I'm the father of them kids in there. Brenda knows who the hell I am, I don't have time for games home boy or whoever you is. I just came to talk to Brenda, see my kids and grandkids, and have a good time this Thanksgiving. I just got out the pen buddy, so you best recognize who you talking about."

Alexis whispered to Brenda. "Ma, I know that voice. He called me the other day. Why don't you just let him in?"

"No, Lexi, we have bigger problems than this. If he finds out that you are not his daughter, he is going to spit fire on all of us." Brenda could barely keep her voice to a whisper, her blood pressure had spiked a bit, and her patience had dwindled.

Pastor Saunders grabbed a hold of Urethra and escorted her to the kitchen. "This is a Carter family matter, not a Saunders family matter. I'm out of it." He threw his hands up and sat down in his chair, he observed the cold of the smothered turkey and other items on his plate. He got up and zoomed to the microwave, turned it on high for two minutes.

"Do you think we should leave?" Urethra asked with a slight fear in her heart, she was unaware of the exact role of the man outside, but from what she had heard, she knew he was trouble.

"No. I don't care who he say he is, he will not disrespect me, or put none of our families in harm's way." His food had finished heating. *That's better*. He thought to himself, as he was ready to chow down, finally he had a chance to enjoy the fruits of his labor, or so he thought.

"Pastor, come here," Brenda yelled out. Everyone in the kitchen was startled at her loud cry for him. Immediately Pastor Saunders and Urethra ran to her assistance.

"What is it Brenda? Is he still out there?" He scanned her face for any sign of crazy.

"Yes, he is still outside my door." Brenda tried her best to speak in a tone that only the four of them could hear, she even signaled for them to step back a little, to at least guarantee that Michael did not hear what they were saying.

"Alexis and I were debating on whether to let him in the house or not. I mean, Sabrina is his child, and it's been years since he's seen anyone of us. He promised good behavior. I told him that if he gave us any sign of trouble if we were to let him in, then I'd have nine-one-one on speed dial." She smirked at the thought of having nine-one-one on speed dial, nevertheless it was the best threat she thought to come up with.

"Well, I don't know about that Brenda, my children are here, too. And as a man of God, I try not to do anything to put my family in more danger than they are already in. And of course, I'm talking about spiritual warfare. We fight not against flesh and blood, but against spiritual municipalities in high places. I don't know what kind of spirit that man has on him right now, especially coming from prison. With all that fussing he's been doing outside, the brotha sounds pretty unstable to me." He paused to look at his wife.

"Furthermore, what happens when he finds out that Alexis is not his daughter? That man will go ballistic on all of us. I just believe that you ought to handle these types of family matters on another day, at least not while my wife and kids are around. Besides, it's Thanksgiving; we don't need to fill our lives with that kind of drama the rest of the day."

Each of them seemed to agree, even Alexis agreed and it was her idea to let Michael into the house. Brenda was very satisfied with what Pastor Saunders had said; they just had to find a way to get rid of Michael, nicely.

Pastor Saunders broke the sudden silence. "I also wouldn't mind mediating at my church or some public place if you like. I don't believe that this type of news should necessarily be told in a private setting where there are many dangers lurking."

"He's not that bad; he never abused or hit me in his life. He ain't no saint, but I doubt that he'll put a hand on me. If he does, I got a machete in the garage that's been waiting for a trial." They each laughed aloud; they knew that Brenda could be both passionate and crazy at the same time. But they also knew that when she said she was going to do something, you best believe that it will be done.

Pastor Saunders waved his hands at the ladies once more to get their attention, "Okay, ladies, enough of this, I'm ready to finish my dinner and warm up my food again." He sighed. "So lets' all do what we have to do to finish the night on a good note. Brenda please do the honors of getting rid of Michael. Alexis and Urethra, you two come with me to the kitchen."

Brenda stepped to the peephole of her big wooden door, and noticed that Michael had vanished. Michael was gone; he was nowhere to be seen. "Well, that was easy," she murmured to herself with glee. Then, she looked outside the window, and still Michael wasn't in sight, just the few bags of junk that was across the street on her neighbors' porch, but Michael was nowhere to be found. She wasn't sure how he actually got to her home because she didn't remember if he drove in a car or not, at least she didn't remember seeing one, either way, the burden that Michael put on them Thanksgiving day, was a burden she was relieved to have to deal with on some other day.

Pastor Saunders pulled Alexis to the side as everyone rumbled around in the kitchen, even Brenda had made it back with the good news, and she was consumed with her food and didn't notice that Pastor Saunders had pulled Alexis to the side.

"Hey, I need to talk to you about this Kita thing, I know that you want your daughter to be with you, but you know how your mother feels about it. Look at Kita, isn't she so... beautiful." He pointed at Kita, a small tear raced outside Alexis's eyes; she saw a reflection of herself when she saw her daughter.

"Well, what do you want to talk about?" Alexis asked inquisitively, she was still a little shaken up on how close she seemed to be to her daughter at that very moment, but yet so far away as well.

"Well, you already know what it is," he said lovingly with all that his heart and soul could muster. He tried his best not to cry, as he observed the triangular build of Alexis's nose and the puffed up cheeks and eyes, which were all a reflection of him. And he being a reflection of his parents and his parents a reflection of their parents, and so on and so forth to the first generation of Adam, a reflection of God. Man, no matter how frail, no matter how sick in spirit, was created in the image of God. God never changes, only man is bound by the seasons of change in his or her life.

Pastor Saunders redeemed his composure. "I love you, Alexis, meet me at the church tomorrow when you get off of work. I'll be there ready and willing to work it out."

With a slight sense of unknowing, Alexis simply said, "Okay." As she settled in her mind. That was the first time she heard Pastor Saunders mention that he loved her. Something about that statement gave her a sense of wholeness, and maybe even a keen awareness for the type of love that she had missed the majority of her life. And that love, was the love of a father, a true father no matter what shape or form he was in, a true father that would love her in spite of her faults and failures. She was excited about the meeting that would take place the next day, she had thought up a few questions for Pastor Saunders, primarily the question of *love* was what had filled her heart.

Loose the Shackles

"**I** do not want to answer another phone call," Alexis whispered under her breath in her tiny cubicle at Sunshine Telemarketing agency. Although the money was good, she had wanted to quit the job for over a month. The only leverage that kept her and all the other drones that worked there was the need to pay rent, lights, insurance and other life expenses. Otherwise, if she were not obligated to such bills, she would have quit the first week.

I hate this job, customer's call here expecting you to give them something. I have never dealt with such rudeness in my life. I mean, my mother could be a female dog at times, but other than that, she's a saint compared to these people. Alexis thought to herself as the digital display was lighting up for her next incoming call.

"Good afternoon, this is Alexis with Studs Electronics, how may I help you?" She wiggled her fingers and looked at the clock, just to take the pressure off the impending complaint she knew was coming.

"Yes, this is Dorothy Mae Wilson, one of my grandkids just bought me one of them HDTV's from your company, and I just can't seem to get it to work. When my grandkids were here the other day, it worked mighty nice, but now that I'm here alone, it doesn't seem like it wants to work for me." She paused for a moment's breath with the user manual in front of her, but with a slight loss of vision, she was barely able to make out the fine print.

She continued. "I told my grandson that I didn't mind my old black and white for the picture show, but that boy insisted on this here television, and it's about to drive me to an early funeral." She said, as her voice was rather soft and a little squeaky.

"Yes, Ma'am, I understand that," Alexis said with a slight grumble. *This is going to be a long conversation.* "Ma'am, what brand of television do you have? So I can look up the user manual for that particular television to point you in the right direction."

The phone was silent for a good five seconds.

"Ms. Wilson, are you still there? What brand of television do you have?" Alexis grudgingly repeated herself. She was ready to throw in the towel at that point.

"Child, I don't know about a brand. I just know that my grandson said that this here thing is some kind of HDTV, and I need to watch my shows, you hear me."

"Ma'am, I surely understand your frustration, but without knowing the brand that makes your television, it's a little hard to help you over the phone."

"Oh, my God, suga, what's the point in calling you people if you can't help out an old lady like me? I told my grandson that I didn't want this here mess, I was satisfied with what I had. That's the problem with ya'll generation today, trying to change things to make them fit your lifetime, while the right thing has always worked. My grandson is no good, I'm missing my shows." Her face was creased with soft wrinkles due to her frustration, and her fingers couldn't keep still over the phone due to her bad nerves.

"Once again, I do apologize," Alexis curtly stated. She wanted to swing on somebody, anybody for putting her on the line with the old lady.

"Yeah, whatever darling, I'll call my grandson in a minute and get to the bottom of this here mess."

That's who she should have been calling in the first place. Old people can surely be a pain in places that even regular grown folks have a hard time talking about.

"Bye, honey," Dorothy Wilson said rather quickly as she hung up the phone. She didn't even give Alexis an opportunity to respond.

Alexis raised her hand to signal her manager for a restroom break, the manager fully arrayed in a black suit, black bow tie, white dress shirt, and black non-name brand shoes trotted over to Alexis begrudgingly as if it was a crime for Alexis to raise her hand, and even prison time to use the restroom.

Alexis managed to keep her composure when her boss met her at her desk with a rugged tone and a look of frustration that would have scared a legion of demons into the swine. "Alexis, what do you want?" he asked sharply. No room for grace uttered from his voice.

Willing and ready to snap, she surprisingly kept her cool a little longer than normal. "I simply have to go to the restroom, boss."

"Well, I 'm sorry Alexis, but you can't take your bathroom break until another five minutes from now, you do know that we are doing power calls right now, right?"

With his non-satisfactory reply to her request, Alexis had had enough and her emotions and bowel movements were at the edge. "Look here, boss man, I'm going to the restroom right now, power calls or not. It's an emergency, and I hope you understand."

And just like that she picked her feet up and placed them firmly on the ground as she waltzed her way to the restroom. *He can fire me, what's the worst that can happen? I sit at home and collect unemployment.*

Her boss was terrified at her clear defiance of him as he saw her backside swing around the corner into the ladies restroom. And then something clicked within him, he was turned on by this young beautiful African-American woman. Not only did she defy his authority, but she walked to the restroom like no body's business. He being a thirty-two year old white male, was a loner, and the last relationship he had, well, let's just say he couldn't remember.

He walked away from Alexis desk, as he tried to contain the feelings that ravished his insides, he contemplated whether to let her go because of the disrespect that she had shown him, or should he keep her on for the purposes of good eye candy.

Alexis exited the ladies' room with the anticipation of returning to her desk as usual. "This white boy is still at my desk, what does he want?" She mumbled under her breath, she just knew that it couldn't be good. "Well, I guess, he's going to fire me, oh well." She grunted as she was just a few feet away from her manager's presence.

Her manager stood next to her desk at six feet two inches tall with a grimacing look on his face, Alexis could not fully read into her boss's composure, but she just knew that something was about to go down as she finally was fully in his presence.

"Listen, Alexis, both you and I were wrong in the way that we handled your situation." He let out a brief smile, as Alexis was stunned in the same manner. She had never heard her boss admit that he was wrong, for all she knew he was a stuck up prick that had no life and wanted to go after everyone that got in his way.

Her boss continued, as if he relived a heavy weight. "I did not realize the severity in your having to use the restroom, and for this I apologize." He abruptly left her desk after that statement, as Alexis questioned the nature of her boss. His reaction and apology almost made her want to go to the ladies' room again, but she decided against it and held her ground. She quietly moved her chair from under her desk and placed her headphones on to accept more calls. *I guess this means I get to keep this raggedy ole' job, I was hoping that he fired me.*

"Thanks for calling Studs Electronics, how may I help you?" Alexis asked with caution, she hoped that the person on the other line couldn't hear her lack of enthusiasm for the work place.

"Yeah, you already know who this is, I just want to get to the bottom line of everything." A familiar voice was on the line, it nearly startled Alexis.

"Listen, here, you can't keep calling my job like this. I can get in trouble for personal calls." She was frustrated and ready to press the red button that was lit up on her computer. But just as soon as that thought migrated in her mind, another thought had formed, a thought of compassion and hope for the man she believed to be her father. She felt a sudden urge to help him, the same type of urge that entered her mind on Thanksgiving Day to let him in the house.

"I just want to know who is that man who's been up in there with ya'll, and why your mama ain't returning my calls?" He sighed, as he flipped through the pages of the photo album of his girls, he basked in the joy in all the years he missed. He had no clue that Alexis was not his daughter, so the joy in seeing them through the years in pictures was something he always held onto. His living arrangements were with an old girlfriend that he barely liked, they each shacked up together at her rundown apartment building near downtown Miami. His girlfriend had two kids of her own, Michael Lewis always questioned if one of the boys were his. Either way, he did not push the issue; he hoped that his girlfriend wouldn't file for a paternity test, which could have led to child support if one of the boys was his.

While the children he conceived with Brenda, at least Sabrina for better words, he figured that there was something increasingly special about them, Brenda was also his first love, and Sabrina was his first-born.

"Michael, honestly, I have nothing to say about the man who you are referring too. All I'm going to say is this. That man is a preacher and he's been helping ma out for a while. The man is married, so don't trip. Anyway, you just need to talk to ma because she got stuff to tell you and I got to go." She remembered that she had her appointment with Pastor Saunders; she just knew that she couldn't be late.

"I have an appointment to make, I'll talk to you later, Michael, bye." She pressed the red button and was immediately disengaged from the conversation. She hated to be rude, but she knew that Michael Lewis would have kept her on the line for another fifteen minutes. She picked up her bags and clocked out, all at the comforts of her desk.

*****

"I'm sorry that I'm late Pastor Saunders, work and traffic was quite stressful." Alexis glanced over at him; she waited for him to ask her to be seated in his pristinely decorated office. He had the usual religious decorum, a four-foot wooden cross hung behind his desk on the wall, just a few feet above his head. His office was also laced with candles, and paintings lining the other three corners of the room. He had the traditional footprints in the sand pictured on his wall to the left and an acrylic painting of 'black Jesus' at the center of his wall before him. It was specially placed there so that every time Pastor Saunders would look up, he would see the image of 'black Jesus', a sign and symbol of humility.

Although the Pastors' decorations were comforting and a sight to see, they ignored the very principles found in Exodus chapter twenty, verse four through six, which was the second commandment, which warranted man to not make any graven images of God.

Yet while Pastor Saunders and religious relics alike may hound down on the other commandments visited in the book of Exodus, they generally lined their sanctuaries with every type of image of God, which is in its own decree not a true representation of God because no man has seen God and lived. Therefore, the images being displayed were a beautiful representation of another god, not the true God that Christians and those alike profess to serve.

"You may be seated, Alexis, I was just reading a few Scriptures here." He looked on at her with love and cheer. His compassion for his eldest child could be seen past his pastoral position; at his core, he was just another father, willing to help his child.

Alexis felt comfortable; all the nervousness had passed away. "You know that you can call me Lexi, everyone calls me Lexi." She smiled, trying to make small talk, all the while trying to figure out exactly what this particular meeting was all about.

"And you can just call me Malcolm, I wouldn't expect for you to call me dad, but that option is also on the table." He hinted, as he closed his Bible for a quick second to play the role of 'dad' and not 'pastor.'

"Okay, I'm cool with that, so what is this meeting all about?" She twirled her fingers as a way to distract herself for what was to come, for she partially discerned the truth, but did not want to believe it. She knew in her heart that that meeting was going to be about her sexuality, but she just had to hear it for herself.

Pastor Saunders had paused; he knew that he had to find the right words to conjure in order to not hurt the feelings of his only daughter, a subject that he had to get used to. "Alexis, your mother and I love you very much, and with that in mind I just wanted to have an intimate conversation with you about your sexual choices," he said as he loosened his black and red striped tie, and then he unfastened the very first button of his white long sleeve dress shirt. He wanted to be comfortable, and have Alexis feel comfortable as well.

Alexis shared a smile; she released her moist rose pink lips, then like clockwork she began to speak. "Well, I kind of knew that you wanted to speak to me about my sexuality, what can I say, my life is like an open book. Everyone knows that I prefer women over men, and right now I'm not planning on changing that. In my opinion, I was born this way.

Why else would I have massive cravings for the female species?" She looked up to breathe; it gave Pastor Saunders just enough time to interject.

"How do you intimately feel about women, what is it that gives you the strong desire to be with a women?" he asked with love, he hoped not to push the envelope too far with his daughter. He knew that he still played both roles of pastor and father; he himself was also accountable to God for the words that he would address with Alexis, and the lifestyle she had chosen.

"Like I said before Malcolm, I believe that I was born this way, somehow somewhere the chromosomes got mixed up and had me liking women." she became slightly defensive. "The craving for a woman is like the lighting of a good smoke, her presence is intoxicating."

Pastor Saunders was blown away by her last statement, his eyes lit up; it forced his brain to think about his own relationship with the woman of his life, his wife Urethra. Although he still loved her very much, the fire that once lit up so brightly, had kindled into something, which could barely be seen. Maybe this conversation with Alexis was just the spark he needed in order to relish his own relationship.

"Malcolm, are you okay?" Alexis noticed that he had veered off mentally.

"Yes, I'm okay Alexis, please do continue." He smiled, and he felt a little embarrassed within himself.

"I'm just saying, when I'm in a relationship with a woman, we are making love, just by the way we look into each other's eyes. As we search within ourselves for those forbidden and hidden places, we find ourselves as one with the other, surfing landscapes of the universe that one would not know unless they had this type of good loving. A woman can give the best expressions of love and lust that a man can't, while her sexual releases are unlimited. With just the glance of her breast and the soothing sensations of her---" She was embarrassed to say anymore. Meanwhile, Pastor Saunders was in awe, he just couldn't seem to get his mind off his wife, which was a good thing. But Alexis could discern that his heart was not fully focused on her situation, and that for Alexis was a little disheartening.

"Well, that's it; I don't have anything else to say." She looked off at his wall, which held the footprints on the sand. *If only my life can be like that right now, like footprints put into the sand by an invisible man. If only life worked that way, I'd be invisible all the time.*

Filled with a little disappointment, but taking on the responsibility that it could be his fault, Pastor Saunders opened his mouth to move forward with the next stage of their conversation. "Alexis, why do you feel that you have this deep rooted lust for women, also where is it written in the word of God that you were born that way?" He caught himself; he realized that he might have pushed a button too soon. So he gently backed away as he eyed her to see her reaction.

Her composure did not change a bit, but on the inside Alexis was boiling with anger. She was tired of explaining herself to people.

"Pastor Saunders, whoops, I mean Malcolm, I crave after women like nobody's business. It's like there is some kind of gravitational pull that a female has on me that honestly sometimes I really can't explain. I crave everything about a woman, not just the sex, but the intimacy drives me wild." She licked her lips as she thought about Karen; she was ready to devour her.

With the feeling that he was sure to lose the uphill battle, he was determined to try to meet Alexis at least half-way on the situation. Not to compromise what the word of God said, but to be able to come to an agreement on the issues, especially the issue of parental rights.

"I'm going to be real frank and candid with you right now, my daughter." He paused for a brief second; he knew that he had to be careful with the words he chose.

"Alexis, my dear daughter, do you even want to be straight?" He looked her dead in the eyes for the first ten seconds that Alexis's head was up and not looking at the top of the desk with her head down.

Alexis stared at him like a deer in the headlights, for she knew that, that particular question would have been asked. In fact, she rehearsed her answer in her car on the way to the church. But what she did not rehearse for, was the love and compassion which backed his words. Everything about Pastor

Saunders composure exemplified that of great love from a father. Perhaps she was overwhelmed.

After one long minute, Alexis broke her silence. "Well--um---I guess I kind of want to like um---go back to being straight. But the raw sensuality of a females touch is overwhelming man. I mean I could pretend all day in this church that I'm going to be straight and I'm going to do right, but who am I kidding. I'm a ride or die chick, and I love me some dikes."

Pastor Saunders still kept his composure, he did not rush to judgment, he did not readily whip out his Bible to the book of Leviticus chapter twenty verse thirteen, no he continued to show love, even in what he would later describe as having a reprobated mind.

"What was your first sexual experience like?" He dug deep, but he knew that he needed to get to the bottom of what was going on with Alexis. He wanted her to be free.

Alexis mentally crawled back into her shell; she wondered if she should share with her father and pastor her sexual escapades. "My first sexual experience was with Kita's father, Ricky Wilder. Back then, he was the love of my life, and after him taking my virginity, I felt both like a woman, and like a bag full of guilt. Now Ricky is a dead beat with two other kids, he still living in the projects. He prides himself on taking advantage of women. I don't even want to talk about that nigga. Oops, I'm sorry Pastor Saunders."

"It's cool." He giggled a bit, "Remember, you can call me Malcolm. Please do continue." He lifted his finger for her to speak.

"That's it, I don't have anything else to say," she said self-consciously.

"Well--" he paused, "What about your first relationship with a woman."

"It was electric, it was like electricity rolling through every part of my body, I swear, Malcolm, if I was a few feet away from anyone else, they would have been electrocuted. The love making was exhilarating, it felt like I was smoking the best green because I thought I was on a high that I could not get off of." Her mind wandered as she licked her lips, she hoped that maybe a fine woman would have opened the door to Pastor Saunders office.

"To tell you the truth, I don't think that I'm going to change, I love the cuda too much to want to be with a man."

Her last statement raised Pastor Saunders eyebrows, as he shifted in his seat after he heard that, he opened up his Bible and was ready to let the spirit of God take over and minister to him the correct words to say to his fallen child.

Alexis noticed the slight tension in her father's forehead, so she sat back in her seat, she also noticed him open his Bible as well, and she was ready to go on the defense.

"Thank you for sharing, Alexis, and I am one to understand what happens when passions take over and we put the Holy Spirit on the back burner. Our passions aren't always a bad thing. There are many who have an extreme passion for Christ, others may have a passion for writing, I have a passion for preaching. But while in my youth, I had some very lustful, provocative passions, which made me do things for which I should have never done. My passions were not for the good of God's Kingdom; as a matter of fact they were for the opposite." He spoke to her in the best tone he knew how.

He lowered his shoulders and continued, "I guess all I am saying is this; your passion for women is that which should only be natural for a man. Your desires although very strong, they are not correct, and are not a part of the very nature for which God has created you to be. It is without a doubt that we as human beings can share and live with many passions, but the passions for that which is unseemly, not only robs God of what he has designed for you His created, but it also takes away the true dignity and truth for who you are as a vessel." He stopped; he noticed that Alexis was burning to ask a question.

"But how could our passions be so wrong when I was born this way? Now I know that not every woman have passions for another woman, but I think that God made me with some sort of chemical imbalance that may have given me more testosterone than estrogen which like makes me want women more. You know what I'm saying?"

"Baby--- I understand what you are saying, I know how hard this must feel for you. But truth of the matter is this, God does not make any mistakes,

He's made you to be a woman. Look at you. Your very DNA says woman. Every organ in your body, every part of you was designed for the fulfillment and procreation of mankind. Think about your daughter, Kita, she lives with us, not once has she mentioned having a liking for a woman. This here lifestyle Alexis, this lifestyle is a lie. It's a stronghold and, unfortunately, God has given you over to a reprobated mindset because you can't see beyond the feelings."

Alexis broke down crying, not all at once, but each tear fell one by one in silence. She cried because she remembered Pastor Saunders preaching on a *reprobate mindset,* and she just knew that it couldn't have been her to have such a thing. She began to consider that her father was judging her; the humility in it all was overwhelming.

"Well, if that's how you feel, then so be it. Don't judge me. God knows my heart, and he is the one that made me this way. So how could my passions be so wrong, when my DNA was changed at birth?" She questioned abruptly, she wiped the tears from her eyes in the process, she was furious.

Pastor Saunders kept his cool, he knew that moment was coming; he practiced everything in his car on the way to church while listening to Donnie McClurkin's 'We Fall Down.' But the pain in his daughters' eyes did not prepare him for that moment, his spirit was troubled, and truth be told, he did not have the right response to say, but he knew that he served an on-time God, and that was all he needed.

God does not need rehearsal or a dress shoot for what he had already spoken into existence, all God really needed was for the pride of man to let his or her guard down and ask Him who created him (man or woman) to supply that particular need.

With a quick change in the atmosphere, Pastor Saunders grabbed Alexis' hand. "Baby, let's pray. Dear heavenly father, I pray for this kindred spirit. Your child, Lord God, I pray that you strengthen her to walk in the right direction, and loose the demons, which have been planted in her life to consume her soul. Dear Lord God, I pray that you show her the right way to live and I pray that the desire for men be at an increase so that this beautiful daughter of yours and mine can see the truth in your being. I pray this prayer in Jesus name, to loose the shackles and set her free, in Jesus Holy name I pray. Amen."

"Amen," Alexis said as she pulled away from his hands and rushed out of his office, not even to say goodbye. She had enough, the spirit of God was working on her, and she knew it. But her desires to believe what she believed, was too much to think that God could have done any different from what He had already done.

"I was made to love woman, I know that's in my DNA," Alexis said to herself as she pressed the unlock key to her blue four door two-thousand and ten Ford Fusion. She sped east on the expressway on her way home to make it on time for her other appointment. The appointment for which she had been craving all day, it was her appointment with her beau, Karen. And with the way she felt between her thighs, she knew within herself that she was not living a lie.

Still Struggling

*I*t's never easy when it comes down to making a change. I wish I hadn't met with my father on yesterday; at least I could still appreciate to live a lie. I figured that our meeting was going to end up about my sexuality, one way or the other, but what I didn't know was that the spirit of God was going to show up and show out on me. Lying up with Karen last night gave me nothing but a sense of guilt and betrayal. I felt like that little girl again when I was caught with my best friend Sylvia. They say that two wrongs don't make a right, but I can't explain why else would I struggle with this? Why else would I feel so passionate for a woman?

You know the book of Genesis talks about how God roamed over the darkness, and the darkness being ruled over by the day, which is the light of the sun. My father talks about this lifestyle like the creation of this world. Maybe what I am is just a shadow of God's glory, a shadow of His image, for who I truly am supposed to be is hidden behind my strong desires, my passionate lust, and my quick arousals at the twitch of a females nipples.

Maybe, just maybe, my darkness is a construction of what could never be good in me; maybe my darkness is a shadow of my past hurts, and the demons for which I struggle with. I know that this lifestyle is not right. But does it make it wrong to have same sex attractions. Is it wrong for another man to kiss another man on the lips while exchanging their oral essences? Is it so wrong for a female to embrace the other in love while holding hands in the park?

Why can't I cuddle up with Karen, why are my flaws looked at greater than the next person? Why does religion get to determine who I sleep with? Why can't God pardon me for how I feel? He did create me; the pastor said that God knew me before I was even born.

God had to know that I would go through this moment. He had to know that I would be screwed up by men, raised by a prostitute and asked to be a good girl. God had to know, and since he already knew me, why didn't he change me? Why didn't God change me at the time of conception? If I was destined to be a boy, God had every opportunity to change me, correct me. But He didn't, He didn't do it.

So, I'm stuck here in this body, questioning the very nature of my being. Questioning the very gene pool for which I was born. Maybe just maybe being a woman was what God had intended for me to be all along. But if this was His intention and I am His creation, why do I feel like I am mentally and sexually flawed. Why do I feel like I'd rather hold onto and caress the warm intricacies of a female's vagina than the flaws of a man's penis?

Why do I feel like the ground is about to shake underneath me when Karen and I are together? There has to be an answer. I just want God to be real with me. Tell me himself that I am living a lie. Tell me himself that my feelings for another chick will send me to hell. I want God to tell me that what I'm doing could never get me through the pearly gates. If I was fully created in God's image, why wasn't I born to be a man?

Journey to Freedom

"**H**ello--- hello is this Sylvia?" Alexis questioned with a partially frightened voice, she shook under her covers; she had a horrible dream, which woke her from her sleep. Karen was cuddled next to her and snored louder than a fat man snored, she was unmoved by Alexis's sudden movements. Alexis knew that Karen wouldn't have understood her dream. She knew that at least her father, Pastor Saunders or maybe even Sylvia would have understood the darkness that consumed her dream.

Angels and demons were in the corners of her brain, unseen images that seemed to be so real. The fear was more than enough to wake her from her slumber. The only problem was she didn't immediately remember where she had placed Sylvia's number, and she surely was not ready for a sermon from her father.

Finally, she found Sylvia's number, and then she immediately dialed it on her cell phone.

"Yes, this is Sylvia, who is this?" She was startled by the call, she recognized the area code, but was not cognizant of who it was since she had barely woke out of her sleep.

"Gurl, this is Lexi, I kind of had this bad dream tonight, and I needed someone to help explain this stuff to me." She left from under the covers, she didn't want to wake Karen, so she lowered her voice and tiptoed to the living room.

"Okay, so tell me about this dream of yours that got you all spooked." Sylvia turned on her bedside lamp, and then reached for her Bible.

"There was like these large thirty-foot or so Angels, I mean they were giants. They were battling these creepy monsters looking things; I mean things that you barely see in horror movies. But the monster looking things had these big long faces, and sharp teeth. At first I thought the big Angels were like the good guys because they were fighting and winning against those sharp toothed monsters, the monsters almost looked like trolls, but worse. But after the big Angels had fought the monsters, they turned around and looked at me, but something was dark, something was sinister about them. I just had a feeling that they were evil as well, and that's when I woke up." She caught her breath, as she analyzed the darkness of the living room, she was painfully afraid.

"I have never had a dream like that before, I nearly wet my clothes." Alexis paused for a response. *What does this all mean?* She shook her head as she reached for the lamp to the left of her sofa. She was happy to be illuminated by the light of the bulb, it instantly ceased the darkness and held the darkness captive for as long as she kept on the light.

"I hear you." Sylvia reluctantly gave a three-word response, she prayed within herself for an answer to her friends dream.

"So what do you think this all means, Sylvia?" Alexis grew impatient, she wanted some immediate answers, and there was a fear inside her that she never felt before.

"I think that it means that there is a battle for your soul, even demons are fighting each other for you. This is surely not a good thing. You know God often speaks to us through dreams and visions. This dream can come as a warning for your life." Sylvia said with love, she didn't want to come across as being preachy, but she wanted to communicate the seriousness in what she had interpreted.

Alexis was a little dumbfounded with the words that Sylvia had spoken, she wanted a little more clarity. "But why would they be fighting over me. I'm nobody's preacher; I'm not in some high place of authority. I guess I just don't get it, besides it was just a dream." She tried her hardest to brush it off, but the fear didn't let her resist the realities for which Sylvia had spoken into her life.

"STOP right there, Lexi, this is not just some lame dream. I believe that this dream is what's really happening in your life. And no, you are not a preacher, but you have a soul. The enemy is warring for your soul. God made mankind to be a unique and special creature, the devil's been mad at this ever since. It gives him and his legions of demons great pleasure to work to kill and destroy you. One of the best ways that the devil accomplishes his mission is through confusion. He often suggests things that are not real, so he basically, plants these questions of doubt in your mind that often are meant for evil doing." She stopped; she didn't want to overwhelm Alexis with too much information for one night.

"I'm scared." Alexis confessed.

"Well, you should be scared, but let's talk tomorrow because there were a lot of things that I had to go through in order to walk in my deliverance. I know you might not be open to hearing this right now, but that lifestyle of lesbianism brings on these familiar spirits. These particular spirits that you have visualized in your dream are after you. Of course, it's not just lesbianism that brings on these types of familiar spirits. There's lust, greed, fornication, adultery and the list goes on, but in my experience and from speaking to some ministers of the cloth, they have recognized that lesbianism can sometimes bring on even stronger, bigger demons."

"It can't be, I have never seen or dreamed anything like that before, no girl has ever come up to me with razor sharp teeth trying to get my digits." She tried her best to comfort herself, she knew that something within her was off balance, and maybe, just maybe, that dream could have in fact been a message from God. "This is some crazy talk, Sylvia; there is no way in the world that I can be under attack by some so called demons. I'm not a bad person."

"Living a lifestyle of lesbianism is not about good or bad, Lexi, it's about what's right before the eyes of God. The main thing to know is that God loves you, and he cares about you. He doesn't love you no less because of what you are going through, in fact, Scripture says that the Angels in heaven rejoice for the one that receives salvation. You are the apple of His eye and all He wants is a solid relationship with you. And I'm not just talking about going to church and following some religious tradition, I'm talking about giving Him some back bending praise. Loving Him more than anything else that you could possibly imagine loving, loving Him even more than Kita."

"So---you mean to tell me that God is not mad at me for being the person that I am, I mean, I do want to change." A tear had shed; she shook her head as she thought about Karen that was fast asleep and naked in her bedroom. "I do have a genuine desire deep within my heart to be straight, but it's so hard, Sylvia. It's hard, and it seems like every time I have even attempted to leave this lifestyle, the pull has gotten stronger and stronger on me. People may judge me, but they don't know my story." She stared across the living room and reminisced on her many sexual encounters with both women and men; she knew that fornication no matter the gender was equally bad before the eyes of the Lord.

"Listen, gurl, I can't sit here and tell you how God feels about your specific lifestyle. That's between you and Him, but I can tell you that according to His word, He wants all of us to see the goodness of His glory. He wants all of us to enter into His gates with thanksgiving and be greeted by an unforgettable praise. He wants us all to be with Him because whether its heaven or here on earth, wherever God is, is where we need to be."

"But what about those demons you were talking about?" Alexis questioned.

"They have no power over you for as long as you believe in the word of God, take up your cross, and follow the one true king."

"If it sounds so easy, why is it so—hard to do? I go to church, but I barely pay attention. My father preaches about the cross, but I'm sure as all get out that I'm not ready to take up my individual cross. Being with a woman feels too good. There is nothing in this world that can satisfy me like a woman, and so there is my battle, there is my tug of war within me. That's why I'm dying to be straight, too. Because on the inside, I know what's right and wrong, but what's wrong feels so good. I didn't choose this life. This life chose me. Dealing with a few bad men is enough to make any girl switch teams." She smiled internally.

"Hey—at the end of the day, Lexi, it's ultimately your choice. I'm not here to point the finger at you, just here to hopefully lead you in the right direction. I will agree with you, getting out of that lifestyle is hard as the gates of hell. Something about being with the same sex just made me want to sink my teeth in sin even more. When I first got up to college, I was loose. I mean, I entertained group sex, participated in many orgy parties and engaged in unprotected sex with both woman and men. I was wild, and I loved every bit of what I did because it felt good. It felt right to me, but all along there was a tugging on my spirit, and never to this day could I shake the look that was on my mother's face when she caught us two in bed together when we were younger."

Alexis grew agitated." So what are you trying to say?"

"What I'm trying to say is that I'm here for you. I'm here to pray with you, study the Bible with you, whatever it's going to take to help set you free. Freedom is a journey, it does not come easy, unless God just wills for it to happen like that."

"So—even if I decided to give this all up and turn back to having a desire for men, could I truly be set free? I mean like, is this something that really happens to folks. I mean you said that you have been set free and all but you're my friend and it's just kind of difficult for me to accept it as that, especially since we've had some history together. So I guess my real question is this, can a person like be like set free from this lifestyle forever without any turning back or something."

"Yes, I believe that a person can be set free forever without turning back, for as long as they keep their heart and mind on God and die to the flesh daily. I won't pretend to tell you that this journey towards freedom will be easy, but it will be right. As my literature class taught me about Robert Frost, there are always two roads to travel. The road to righteousness is always the road less traveled by. But this is the road that I have elected to travel because this is indeed the road that leads to eternal life with Jesus Christ."

"I would like to take that road, but I'm just not sure if I'm ready. Yes, I want to be straight, but it comes at a cost of me giving up all of my pleasures in life. What's this life to live if there is no fun in it?" Alexis looked down at her phone, she had been talking to Sylvia for a good hour and thirteen minutes, her phone got hot.

"I understand, Lexi, this moment right now may not be your time, but I believe that your time for freedom will come sooner than you think. I had the same mentality, but because of the grace of God and some good people I met at my church in Chicago, I have never been the same. Of course, I'm not saying that I don't deal with temptation; I deal with it all the time on both sides of the fence. But because of my relationship with Christ, I am able to better manage my sinful nature. Anyway, Lexi, I am dead tired," she paused. "I need to get some sleep. Are you cool with that? Are you going to be alright?"

"Yeah, I'm good, have a good night." Alexis hated to end the conversation. She wished that she could have spoken to her friend all night; there were many questions that she had for Sylvia that were left unspoken.

*****

"Hey, what's up, Lexi, you're not going to work today?" Karen asked with her face drenched with a cold sweat, she also wrestled some demons that night, but demons of a different kind. She just couldn't shake the liquor, which consumed the deepest parts of her digestive system. She had a slight hangover.

"I don't feel so good, gurl. I already called in sick; I think I'm about to smoke a blunt or something to kind of calm my nerves.

"What's wrong?" Karen had a startled delay in her voice. "I heard you when you got up last night and went to the living room."

"Nothing, I'm cool," Alexis said with a half-smile.

"Alright fine, you don't have to tell me. On second thought, who were you talking to on the phone that late in the morning?"

This girl is so nosey, why can't she just leave me alone and chill?

"It was nobody, Karen." Alexis snapped. "I'm going outside to relieve some of this pressure."

"Okay, suit yourself," Karen said without a fight, "but when you come back in, we will have to talk."

"Yeah, whateva, gurl." She stretched her legs to the floor, then headed to the restroom to wash away both the fear she felt and her early morning cold in her eyes and the slightly caked up white circular ring that had formed around her warm lips.

Maybe it was just a dream; I hope that Sylvia wasn't right. I hope that all is well with my life.

Alexis regained her composure and headed to the front door of her apartment, with the beautiful sunshine that waited for her attention; she released the knob and pulled out one of her favorite past times, another *Black&Mild*. She inhaled one good time, and then warmly blew it back out. She felt good all over again as she observed the many cars passing by her apartment. She always enjoyed the second floor view, and the safety she felt that it brought her. But no particular floor or key or locked door would have been able to protect her from the realm of evil that was destined to consumer her.

Alexis was satisfied with her smoke retreat, she received in herself a renewed confidence and pleasure. The fear which hunted her the night before had all but disappeared, and she was ready to spend time with her girlfriend, Karen, both above the sheets and under the sheets, no matter what the warning from her dream had described, Alexis chose sin over salvation.

Lord God, how can I do this again? I confessed to Sylvia how much I want to be straight, but the tug of war for unadulterated pleasure has consumed me once more. Help me Jesus; help me to one day be free.

Covered By the Blood

"**S**ylvia, it happened again." Alexis screamed through the earpiece.

"What? What are you talking about, and why are you calling me at three in the morning again?" Sylvia rushed to turn on her bedside lamp, her soon to be fiancé was over her apartment for the night, and she woke him up. She grabbed her Bible and headed to her living room. She wasn't sure what to say.

"Listen, Sylvia, I had another one of those dreams, but this time it was worse. Remember one of those big Angels that I was telling you about? Well, it grabbed me and began gnawing on my leg. And as it gnawed on my leg, it waited til' my leg healed, and then it started to gnaw on it again. It was just a continuous cycle, and then I heard people screaming all around me. People were coming down from some tunnel looking passageway. It all creeped me out, this is no joke. Tell me what's up. Tell me how to get rid of these dreams, tell me, please."

"Let's pray. Are you open to that?" Sylvia asked nervously, out of fear that her friend wasn't going to be receptive to her initiation of prayer. She held her Bible even tighter to her chest, she knew and understood the significance for her friend to be set free. She also understood that like spirits would try to latch itself onto her if she wasn't careful. That's why she knew that the best remedy to remove the demonic forces was to pray and to be covered by the blood of Jesus.

"Yes, that's cool; I'll do anything to shake these dreams." She was indeed nervously shook up; she was in panic mode as she spoke in the small confines of her bathroom. She did not want to wake up Karen, but she probably already had with her loud scream.

"Dear heavenly father, we thank you for your wonderful grace, we thank you for your love, Lord God. Lord, this here is your daughter who is struggling with something that can be cured, and that cure is deliverance. So father I just pray that you intercede in her life in a miraculous way. Break the chains of addiction, Lord. Break the chains of lesbianism; break the chains of lust, Lord, so that the enemy has no place to stay in her life." She paused for a moment to catch a quick breath; she remembered the many prayers that were prayed over her life. The many women in her church up in Chicago that laid hands on her shoulder, she remembered the oil that blessed her head and the tongues that were spoken for her own deliverance.

Sylvia continued with her prayer. "Dear Lord God, we pray that this demonic realm that has set forth to latch itself on her life. That it cease and decease, Lord. We pray that it cease and decease so that it has no more power over your daughter, Lord God. And father I just pray that you cover Alexis in your blood, Lord God. Cover here with the blood of Jesus; renew in her a right mind and a right spirit Lord. Lord, we know that it's not just lesbians and homosexuals that are struggling Lord, we know that there are sinners out there with great iniquities. So Lord God, I just pray that you show your love for this fallen spirit. Restore and renew her Lord, make her whole. Have her to commune with you in the right way. Make her walk a walk of joy and peace, not a walk of hardship. Renew in me a right spirit Lord; keep me away from the seat of the sinners and the hearts of the scornful." Sylvia gave her all as she gripped the phone even tighter.

"Help her, Lord God, help and heal my best friend, Alexis, Father help her to be a Psalm chapter one verse one through six type of person. These things I ask in Jesus name, amen."

Alexis stood still in silence. She wondered if the truth that her father spoke of was real, she wondered if maybe her lust for women was a strong hold. Her mind had gone in a different direction; she questioned what it meant to have a reprobated mind.

Alexis was tired of fighting, she was tired of not declaring what she truly knew which was hidden deep within her heart. It was a declaration that predated Ricky Wilder, Karen, and Sylvia, her true declaration which was always there at the very core of her existence.

Alexis couldn't stand the silence any longer; there was a boiling up in her spirit that she could not explain. The warmth had draped her body and pulled on her stronger than any sin that she had committed. Her hands shook repulsively, she was barely able to grip the phone, but she knew that the feeling she felt was out of this world. It was almost as if she wasn't herself anymore, she didn't understand what was happening, but remembered the times she saw fellow church members going up to the front of the church with a similar experience. And just like clockwork without any coaching or premeditated script, what came out of Alexis's mouth would set the precedence for who she would work to become from that day forward.

"I, Alexis Carter, want Jesus to be in my life, I want him to make me whole. I want him to set me free. I want to be covered by the blood of Jesus!" She loosened her grip of the phone as she involuntarily raised her hands towards the heavens. God was truly working on her in a powerful way. Her phone had broken on the tile bathroom floor and shredded into a million little pieces. Alexis wept as she took to her knees to gather the pieces that were loosed on her newly defunct phone. Each piece she picked up and threw away picked up and threw away, a symbol of the old pieces of her life that were working for something new.

Sylvia couldn't hardly believe the confession she had heard over the phone. She was elated. Of course, when she tried to call Alexis back, the automated voicemail responded.

"Thank you, Lord God, for saving your daughter, now the hard part begins." Sylvia cried tears of joy for her friend and was ready to do a victory chant, till she remembered that her fiancé to be was in the bedroom fast asleep.

Being saved is only the beginning to the walk of a lifetime with God. Sylvia thought to herself as she remembered how difficult it was for her to take each step towards her own freedom. She had many victories and disappointments when she took that journey to be straight.

Epilogue: The Walk

"**M**erry Christmas, Malcolm." Brenda welcomed Pastor Saunders in her home with cheer. It was Christmas day, Pastor Saunders brought over his whole family just as he did on Thanksgiving.

"Merry Christmas, Brenda." Malcolm blushed, he barely noticed the slight scorn, which eluded Urethra's face.

"Merry Christmas, Alexis, Kita, Sylvia, Sabrina, Brandy, Urethra. Merry Christmas Michael, Jason, and Karen," Brenda had said.

"Merry Christmas, Brenda," They each said on one accord as Kirk Franklin's *There's No Christmas Without You* was on loop in Brenda's Bose CD Player.

The house was decorated with the usual red and green Christmas décor, while the Christmas tree was filled with wonderful ornaments and a black female Angel marked the top of the tree. Tightly wrapped gifts lined the triangular surface of the tree. The Christmas lights roamed around the tree and moved with the beat of the music being played in Brenda's CD player.

Everyone sat firmly on the couch with casual conversation; they enjoyed each other's company. Sabrina and Pastor Saunders' boys were in Brandy's room playing video games.

"Well, I'm going to break the ice; I still can't get over the fact that Alexis is your daughter, Malcolm."

Michael Lewis shook his head, he reminisced on how he received the news of Malcolm's paternity just two weeks shy of Christmas. It was Alexis's idea to tell Michael so that he could be a part of their Christmas dinner without any drama.

"Yes, it was hard for me, when I found out at first, but I have embraced this fact, and I love her just as much as I love my boys that God blessed me with." Pastor Saunders smiled and held his wife a little tighter than before.

"I will admit though, I was a little mad at first to hear this, but I'm glad that Alexis invited me, and I'm happy to see my baby, Sabrina, is doing well with herself." Michael glanced over at Sabrina, and in his heart, Alexis was still his daughter.

Michael reached for the Welch's sparkling grape juice, he was content, and he craved for that moment, a moment to be amongst family. A moment he never really had the opportunity to have since he was constantly in and out of jail and on the run.

"Karen, I'm surprised to see you here, I know that you and Alexis had broken up," Brenda said with suspicion.

"Yeah, Alexis invited me, of course. She kind of felt bad for me because I don't have any family down here in Miami and all. I mean, I hope you don't mind me being here, I don't want to cause no trouble or anything."

"No, you're okay," Brenda said curtly. *I hope the child ain't bring no demons in here, don't need my child being pulled back deep into that lifestyle.* Brenda sharply thought to herself. But because of a lack of education, she did not realize that it did not take a person to be consumed in lesbianism to be consumed by demons. Her former lifestyle of prostitution brought legions of demons to her former home in the projects, and it latched themselves onto her daughters. No matter the type of sin, it was all spiritual warfare.

"Excuse me---Excuse me." Alexis rose from her seat. "I have an announcement to make, this is my boyfriend, Jason, he's so special to me, we have been dating for like three weeks now, he honors me and is in my corner as I work out my deliverance. He and I met at the burger spot near my job, the moment he asked me for my number when were in line getting a burger, was the moment I remembered that having a desire for a handsome man like Jason wasn't a bad thing. As a matter of fact, I knew that in my spirit, it was the right thing." She gave Jason a quick kiss on his left cheek.

Alexis continued with her testimony. It was an odd thing to do on Christmas day, but she felt that it was the only time she'd be around all of her family in one place.

"All of yawl know how hard these last few months have been for me, and if it wasn't for my conversations with Sylvia over the phone, and the grace of God, I probably wouldn't be where I am today." She looked around at all the smiling faces, she broke down in tears, and Jason held her hand even tighter.

"It's okay, baby, you're doing good." He squeezed her hand a little firmer. Jason was the man who was meant for Alexis, he was smart, handsome, a respecter of woman and loved the Lord. He ministered in his choir at the local church and was pursuing his bachelor's degree in theology. Unlike the life that Alexis lived, he wasn't raised in the projects of Miami, he was raised in the suburbs of Kendall, the area where Brenda resided in their new home. At twenty-two years of age, Jason was quite mature, he had a mindset that quite surpassed the immaturity of his male counterparts. He quickly took a liking to Pastor Saunders, perhaps because he too desired to be a man of the cloth one day.

Alexis wiped her last tear. "I still have a long walk to go on this path towards being straight, it took Sylvia three years. I'm hoping that it takes me less." Everyone cheerfully laughed at her last statement. Each eyed the other.

"Well, I won't say anymore. I'm just happy that Jason has been so understanding of my situation. I guess the greatest gift that I could have ever received this Christmas was the beginning of my deliverance. Sylvia thank you so much, gurl, for showing me by example and in the word of God, what true sexuality is supposed to feel like."

"It's nothing, I have to get on my knees every day and ask God to keep me, but I am stronger now than I have ever been. Freedom feels so good when God gets in the picture." Sylvia gave a quick toast as they all sipped down the Sparkling Grape Juice.

Brenda swelled up with tears on that unexpected announcement; she knew how hard the battle had been for Alexis to work towards being straight.

Pastor Saunders interjected. "You know, Alexis, the walk is always the hardest part about deliverance. Deliverance is a process; very rarely does it all happen overnight. I know that you still have questions; I know that you are still burdened by the thoughts, cravings, and images of being with another woman. But God has made you stronger than those thoughts, he will deliver you completely so that you don't look back like Lots wife did when Sodom and Gomorrah was destroyed."

Pastor Saunders paused for a moment as he looked away from Alexis and on to Karen, he tried to find the right words within himself to say to her. "And Karen, I want you to also evaluate your life, know that God can also tear down those walls of confusion and lies. I want you, Karen, to have a thirst for righteousness. And maybe, you will have a desire for dying to be straight, too."

A Reading Group Guide:

Dying To Be Straight! Too

Michael D. Beckford

Alexis Carter went through mountains of disappointments and trails of sadness on her journey to be straight. Her journey was a constant tug of war between her flesh and her spirit, and it wasn't even until the end of the book that she decided to take the walk with Christ.

Change often happens overtime, rarely is it immediate. We have to be patient with our fellow brothers and sisters that are going through the struggle, no matter what it is. And sometimes the one we struggle with (i.e. Sylvia), may just be the one that helps to set us free.

Discussion Questions

1. There was a particular young lady that Alexis Carter met in the Prologue and parted ways with in the Epilogue. Who was this young lady? And what do you think the significance of her meeting and parting ways with that young lady means to this story?

2. Ricky Wilder had certain plans for his then girlfriend, Alexis Carter. Describe what his true plans were for her.

3. Can you describe the similarities between Michael Lewis and Ricky Wilder? In what ways are they connected?

4. What would you consider Alexis Carter's defining moment in this book?

5. Why did Alexis become so attached to woman? Was it simply because of her being hurt by a man, or was it based on pent up desires that she'd already had?

6. Who was the main character's biological father?

7. In the Chapter **Journey To Freedom** which character made this statement, "Living a lifestyle of lesbianism is not about good or bad Lexi, it's about what's right before the eyes of God. The main thing to know is that God loves you, and he cares about you."

8. The main character's mother, Brenda was a prostitute and had some heavy struggles of her own. Do you believe that her lifestyle played a role on her daughter's bad decisions?

9. In the chapter **Covered By The Blood,** Alexis experienced a second dream that prompted her to call her friend Sylvia. Can you recall exactly what that dream was?

10. Sylvia thought this in the chapter **Covered By The Blood** *Being saved is only the beginning to the walk of a lifetime with God.* Do you believe this to be true?

Take a Quick Look At Michael Beckford's next book in the *Dying to Be Straight!* Series

Dying To Be Straight! Again

Prologue: Confessions

*D*ear Lord God, I have tried to fight the good fight, but this sin continues to strain me. God only you know and understand the pain, anguish for which I go through, and the humility for which I feel in fighting with this degree of confusion. Lord, I pray that you take this away from me for good. Let me not continue to roll around in the mud of destruction and same sex attractions. Lord it is only by your power and your grace that I can operate today, so I pray and ask that you be my guide. Give me your strength. Transform me. Purify me oh Lord. Make me over again. And when all else fails, I will repeat the process, fasting and praying before your throne.

So, here is my confession Lord Jesus, I have been caught up with some men in the wrong places, acting out in some ungodly ways.

Just to keep it real with you Jesus, I kind of like sleeping with men, I indulge in the pleasure of another man taking me to the moon and back. I enjoy the frequencies of our hook-ups and the feel of his six-pack oozing out of his shirt. I lust after the throbbing of his second heartbeat crested between his legs. I enjoy the tender sounds of confidence, knowing that he and I are still men, yet temporary pleasure partners. I relish in the thrill, yet I am saddened by the guilt.

Lord you know that I have traveled this road before, I've been delivered from homosexuality, but now it's reared its ugly head back at me and came back in full force, more powerful than before. I fell like a fraud, a fool because you *have given me the victory, but then a little tiny seed of sin came in and turned into a full-blown tree of destruction. I told everyone of my deliverance and they believed in me, you believed in me. But look at me now God, I'm just a fool playing with time, hoping not to get caught, hoping that the men that I hook-up with through casual connections aren't the same men that I have prayed with and tried to help deliver one time or another.*

So, these are my confessions Lord, will I ever be straight again? Or will my desires for men, outweigh my desires for you? Help me Lord Jesus; I really do want to be free, what is the price that I will have to pay if people really know about me? Will I---

A sudden knock on the door interrupted his prayer.

"Come on in," the man had said, he wished that he wasn't interrupted. He wished that he had a little more time with God in his personal prayer closet.

A young bright-skinned young lady entered into the man's office.

"What is it young lady?" He adjusted his clothing and his mindset, he wished that he didn't have to take on what he knew was about to come next.

The young lady looked around for a second before responding, "Pastor Johnson, it's time for church, the other ministers are waiting for your entry into the sanctuary."

Take The Pledge (I WANT TO BE SET FREE!)

"For whosoever shall call upon the name of the Lord shall be saved."
-Romans 10:13 K.J.V.

Dear Lord God I struggle with this sin, this sin of homosexuality and lesbianism. Lord God I know that you are all powerful and an awesome God, so right now I lay down my life to you. I want you more now than ever. I don't want to be stuck in this lifestyle of homosexuality. Lord God I know that you are greater and you have so much more for me, it is through Jesus Christ that I will be delivered today and I will be set free!

So, I pledge to live a lifestyle of freedom from this day forward, so I can be a champion for Jesus Christ, living a Godly life. Free from homosexuality and lesbianism, free from my addictions. Amen.

Name:

_____

Date:

_____

If you have just taken this pledge then I must say congratulations. God is so good and he can deliver you from anything which you ask of him, there is no problem too big or small for God. Jesus died for every one of our sins including the sin of homosexuality; never feel like it's too late. I know you may struggle like Paul Stringer, but continue to press forward into Christ. Right now is the time to find a good bible based Christian Church if you don't already enjoy a church home. Take this pledge and place it in a secret place, this is between you and God. Then when you feel weak, remember this pledge and lean on God's word which is in the bible, his words precede anything else you could ever read or I could ever write. I love you my fellow brother or sister, but most importantly, God loves you most.

"That if you shall confess with your mouth the Lord Jesus and shall believe in your heart that God has raised Him from the dead, you shall be saved."
-Romans 10:9 K.J.V.

Did You Enjoy Reading Dying To Be Straight! Too?
We would love for you to read more titles by Michael
D. Beckford available on speakpublishing.com and
other fine retailers online and in-stores.

Dying To Be Straight! (Available Now)
Beautifully Ugly People! (Available Now)
I am The Secret! (Available Now)
More Beautifully Ugly People! (Available Now)
Shaniqua is White! (Available Now)
Speak Up! Poetry (Available Now)
Poetry of My Sins! (Coming Soon)
Dying To Be Straight! Again (Available Now)
Straight? (Coming Fall 2017)

www.ingramcontent.com/pod-product-compliance
Lightning Source LLC
Chambersburg PA
CBHW031602240626
47153CB00002B/601